I0590858

THE DECEIVER

TALES OF THE FEISTY DRUID™ BOOK 4

CANDY CRUM

MICHAEL ANDERLE

LMBPN

DISRUPTIVE IMAGINATION

The Deceiver (this book) is a work of fiction. All of the characters, organizations, and events portrayed in this novel are either products of the author's imagination or are used fictitiously. Sometimes both.

Copyright © 2017 Candy Crum, Michael T. Anderle, CM Raymond, LE Barbant
Cover by Mihaela Voicu http://www.mihaelavoicu.com/
Cover copyright © LMBPN Publishing

LMBPN Publishing supports the right to free expression and the value of copyright. The purpose of copyright is to encourage writers and artists to produce the creative works that enrich our culture.

The distribution of this book without permission is a theft of the author's intellectual property. If you would like permission to use material from the book (other than for review purposes), please contact info@kurtherianbooks.com. Thank you for your support of the author's rights.

LMBPN Publishing
PMB 196, 2540 South Maryland Pkwy
Las Vegas, NV 89109

First US edition, October 2017
Version 1.01 January 2019

The Kurtherian Gambit (and what happens within / characters / situations / worlds) are copyright © 2015-2020 by Michael T. Anderle.

DEDICATION

From Candy

To my boys, thank you for
being my reason for everything.
To my family who support me
no matter what.
To the fans and readers--thank you!

From Michael

To Family, Friends and
Those Who Love
To Read.
May We All Enjoy Grace
To Live The Life We Are
Called.

The Undying Illusionist Team

JIT / Beta Readers

Kimberly Boyer
Alex Wilson
Kello ODonnell
Joshua Ahles
Melissa OHanlon
Paul Westman
Micky Cocker

Thomas Ogden
John Findlay

If we missed anyone, please let us know!

Editor
Lynne Stiegler

THE DECEIVER

PROLOGUE

The sun had been bright earlier in the day, the entire sky free of any clouds to hide it. But the closer it had come to mid-day, the more the sky had begun to darken, and the temperature had fallen several degrees as well. It was almost as though the gods knew what was to take place, as if Hell itself were welcoming its newest occupant.

Scarlett watched out the window of the Capitol building as the citizens of Arcadia gathered out front with candles in hand, not that they could be lit now that it was starting to rain. It was turning out to be quite the sendoff.

While she had hated the bitch, Scarlett was painfully aware that some kind of show for the fallen Dean was necessary.

It was important that the city feel Talia had been wrongfully taken from them. It was important that they feel they had lost someone who was vital to their existence. As long as Scarlett played the part well, the city would become angry over the loss, and it would make them more vulnerable to her mystics' influence.

Arcadia's newest Chancellor and her mystic friends had decided that a proper funeral was in order. It would ensure the

1

people would be open to a replacement, and accept the story the group would be handing out.

Straightening her clothes, Scarlett turned from the window and headed toward the door. She took a moment to smile at the bloodstain they had been unable to get out of the floor— the very one that had been left when Talia's head had hit the wood.

A casket had been carefully crafted, the wood expertly carved and stained to a rich, dark color. It had been set up at the top of the Capitol steps, several feet above everyone on the ground below. The symbolism had seemed appropriate to Scarlett.

What no one knew was that Talia's body was nowhere near that casket. Shortly after Scarlett had seen the decapitated corpse in the office, she'd had it carried away and dumped in the tunnels. She found that to be a much more fitting burial for someone as hideous as Talia.

"Are you ready for this?" Nikolai, one of her mystic friends, asked.

Scarlett nodded, a dark smile spreading across her face. "Oh, yes. I've been ready for this for quite some time. Make sure no one gets close to the casket."

Nikolai laughed. "It's been bolted shut. No one is getting in there. I figured the last thing we wanted was anyone popping it open and realizing the bitch wasn't in there."

"Indeed. She's right where she belongs—in the sewers with the rest of the shit. I'm a wonderful actress, but I'm not so sure I'll be able to summon a single tear for her loss. I might even have to use a few tricks." It amused her to talk about Talia in such a way, especially on the day of her funeral.

This was more like a party for Scarlett. An official announcement of her victory. Still, no one else could know that.

Scarlett felt Nikolai brush against her mind, and she could sense his intention. She did not block him, but instead allowed him entrance so he could assist her. Nikolai pushed against her mind, thoughts suddenly overwhelming her and her senses.

She was trapped inside a dark room, her ankles and wrists bound as many of something that felt like needles pressed into her back. The straps were cranked tighter, pulling her harder against the spikes. It felt as though they had pierced the skin and she wanted to scream, but instead her eyes burned as tears began to form.

Scarlett gritted her teeth as the straps were pulled even tighter, and more tears fell down her face. Suddenly, the image was lifted, but the pain still lingered in the back of her mind. Her tears were still flowing, and she realized Nikolai hadn't yet let go of her.

"Very nice," Scarlett said, wiping the tears just enough that they didn't look obvious, but still produced the illusion that she gave a damn. "You had me all tied up, and I thought that was going somewhere fun. Well, it *was* fun, but next time we play, no spikes."

Nikolai shook his head and smiled. "You're relentless, but I like that about you. I'll keep the pain lingering in the back. You only need to call on it when it's needed."

She nodded and grabbed the doorknob, opening it and stepping outside into what was now a rainy day. She focused hard on the pain rooted in the back of her mind to keep her from smiling while she watched the drops fall on Talia's casket. Even without her in it, the sentiment was still there.

Making a good show of things, Scarlett crossed the landing to stand behind the casket, allowing her brows to furrow for the crowd as she laid her hands on the wood. After what she felt had been an acceptable moment of silence, she turned her gaze toward the masses.

"Thank you for joining us today," Scarlett said, allowing the fake tears to permeate her voice. She shook her head. "I'm not even sure where to start."

The faces in the crowd expressed sadness as they watched her put on a show. She could feel the power in the minds of her friends, who were standing with her, as they pushed their influence toward the first few rows of people—the ones who could see her best.

They truly wanted Scarlett to be perceived as a sympathetic, loving leader. Someone who was strong enough to admit her fears, but destroy their enemies.

"As many of you know, Talia and I were very close. We were best friends, even though we had met only recently through the Academy. Getting hired on and being given the chance to help her fulfill her dreams for the school was the best opportunity I have ever received. She was kind and considerate, and she put the needs of others before herself."

The words nearly made her choke, and she felt Nikolai pushing against her a little harder, and the pain his push produced made her squint as she gripped the casket, but the crowd no doubt thought the look on her face was emotional pain.

She took a deep breath and relaxed a bit as Nikolai pulled back. "We all know what happened, but no one has admitted it to you. No one has proclaimed what truly happened here. I will not be that person. I will not stand by silently when something needs to be done. There have been rumors swirling around the city in the last couple days since it happened, but none have been worse than the truth."

Scarlett took a moment to gaze at the crowd as everyone turned to one another, whispering amongst themselves.

"Talia did not die peacefully. There is a reason this casket is closed. Talia was *murdered*. Without a doubt, it was Arryn. She snuck into the city and took the life of the one person who challenged her. Talia knew what she was, as did Amelia, but Amelia had let the power go to her head. She helped Arryn escape the jail, knowing that the fear the girl had caused would keep the city relying on the Chancellor for answers. But Talia knew. Talia discovered what had been happening, and she tried to stop it."

Scarlett stepped out from behind the casket and walked to the edge of the top step. The rain had begun to pour now, and she had to shout louder over the sound of it beating on the cobblestones, the roofs, and the casket behind her.

"Talia had Amelia arrested for murder—the murder of a guard that she herself had employed to protect her. Talia locked her up, but Arryn helped her escape, just as Amelia had helped Arryn not long before. Together, they beheaded our dearly beloved Talia, the woman who stood up for the city when the Chancellor wouldn't, and took on her job. The woman who would have soon led us back to where we need to be. They took her from us, but I won't let that go. I *will* stand up for the city. I *will* stand for what is right. I will stop at *nothing* to get revenge, not only for our city, but for Talia."

Cheers erupted then, the people in front screaming louder and making a bigger show of it than the rest. Slowly but surely, it spread to the rest of the crowd like wildfire. Just as Scarlett and her friends had hoped, the moving speech with the magical push had been enough to secure their loyalty.

Scarlett said her farewells to Talia loudly enough for everyone to hear before leaning over and kissing the casket in front of their expectant eyes. As her mouth hovered just over the wood, she said, "And *that's* how you take a city. Goodbye, you fucking bitch. May you rot in hell."

CHAPTER ONE

Arryn stood at the base of the *Heilig* tree, her hands on her hips as she stared up into its massive branches and thick leaves. She sighed heavily, shaking her head as she tapped her foot.

"Dante, you better get your ass back down here!" she said.

Over the years, Arryn had assisted with the care of the children of the village in one way or another. She had helped feed them, clothe them, bathe them, and did anything else that came along. But none of it had prepared her for this.

The tiger cub was quite a troublemaker. His mother, Snow, had adapted to life in the forest pretty well. The tiger cub, however, was quite the little shit. He had never been around that many trees, and there were so many animals to play with that he had no idea what to do with himself.

His newest favorite pastime was climbing high into trees. But not just any trees—Dante had taken a liking to some of the biggest trees in the forest, including the *Heilig*.

The *Heilig* was the biggest tree in the entire forest. She had once caught a glimpse of what it looked like from above when she had been connected to one of the many birds in the forest. Its branches reached high into the sky, much taller and broader than any other tree as far as the bird could see.

The power the druids put into the tree during their death rituals had created the strongest plant in the forest, possibly the world. And Dante just *loved* to play in it.

"Trouble in paradise?"

Arryn jumped, turning to see Cathillian standing behind her. She sighed and rolled her eyes. "Yes. I don't understand—even though he knows he's going to get stuck, he keeps climbing up there anyway."

Cathillian shrugged. "Sounds like any other kid, only this one is furrier and *way* cuter."

Arryn scoffed. "Furry and cute, yes. Pain in my ass, also yes."

Cathillian took a few steps closer, looking high into the branches. Arryn did the same, finding the young cub swatting at a bird that was flying away, seemingly unamused. He growled at it, but it sounded more like an angry purr than anything. Despite her annoyance, she couldn't help but smile. He was an adorable little bastard.

"Why don't you get Snow to go after him?" Cathillian asked.

Arryn's hands went out to her sides as she looked at him incredulously. When Cathillian just smiled, she pointed behind him. He turned and saw Snow lying there, completely uninterested in any of her cub's shenanigans.

"He does it so much now that she just doesn't give a damn anymore. That, and I think she knows I'll end up getting him down myself. Besides, the last thing I need is his thousand-plus-pound mother getting stuck in the tree along with him."

Cathillian laughed and shook his head. "She's his mom. She has better instincts than you do, no offense. If she's not worried, you should take the hint and not be worried either. He's just a big baby kitty. He likes to climb; it's natural."

Arryn sighed in exasperation. "I thought about that, but then I thought about him losing his grip and falling a couple hundred feet to his death. It almost made me hyperventilate. I just can't do it." Arryn looked at Snow. "You're slacking, *Mom*."

Snow grumbled, standing and leaning back in a big stretch before flopping down on her side and closing her eyes again.

Arryn shook her head. "This is ridiculous."

Another baby roar sounded. The tiger cub pounced onto a different limb when one of the squirrels decided to engage him in play. Arryn rolled her eyes, trying to decide if she was angry about him not paying attention to her or if him playing with the squirrel was too cute to get him in trouble.

"This whole mom thing sucks. I should've picked a bird. They take care of themselves," Arryn said.

Snow lifted her head and growled before flopping her head back down onto her paws.

Dante pounced again, only this time, his back paws slipped off the branch. His body immediately curled around it as he struggled to climb back up, and Arryn jumped, fear taking over as she realized he had been close to falling.

Her eyes flashed green as she threw her hand out, vines sprouting and flowing through the tree before grabbing hold of the cub and wrapping around him like a harness. She slowly lowered him, and she could hear him grumbling his discontent as he descended.

Within moments, the cub was dangling at eye level with Arryn. Once again, her hands came to rest on her hips as she stared him down.

Cathillian laughed again, and her eyes darted over to him, an angry look on her face. "*What* are you laughing at?"

He pointed at her. "You. I'm laughing at you. You've gone from carefree and seeking revenge to being a full-time mom. It's pretty comical."

She gave a sarcastic smile. "That may be so, but I can still kick *your* ass." Arryn turned back to Dante. "And *you*… You need to quit climbing so high into the trees. You're gonna fall and kill yourself."

Cathillian continued to smile at her. "You're a pretty good mom. You know, while you were gone, Celine and Nika both joked about you and me having half-pointy-eared babies."

Arryn finished releasing Dante from his bonds. The cub now safely in her arms, she turned to Cathillian with wide eyes. "Why the *hell* would they do that?"

He suddenly looked very guilty, only shrugging. "I don't know."

Arryn shook her head. "You're no better for even bringing it up. What is the matter with you? You were probably the one who suggested it in the first place. I don't have time for this." She thrust Dante into his arms. "Here, *Dad*, you babysit. I have to go get my ass properly kicked by Nika. I'll be sure to ask her about that little conversation."

Cathillian's eyes widened as he shook his head. "No. Don't say anything about it. *Please*."

Narrowing her eyes, Arryn smiled. "You just don't want her mad at you. You know she would come at you and beat you for real." Arryn laughed hard. "I'm gonna tell her!"

Arryn ran for Snow, quickly straddling her and tapping her on the shoulder as she expected the big cat to save her master in a hasty retreat. The tiger did nothing more than grumble a bit before rolling even farther onto her side, knocking Arryn off-balance.

"Damn," Cathillian said. "That was *some* getaway."

Arryn sighed and poked the tiger in the shoulder. "You're a traitor. You see if I take you fishing anymore."

Arryn stood, gave Cathillian an enthusiastic middle finger, and walked toward the training grounds. She'd been shown up by not one, but *both* her familiars. It was just her luck that she would find two animals that were just as sarcastic and defiant as she was.

AMELIA SLEPT LATE THAT MORNING, having stayed up too late the night before drinking wine with the Chieftain. It was amazing to her now that she had spent her entire life terrified of the druids. She had realized how foolish that was when she'd first met Laurel, the druid from the Dark Forest who had aided them in the battle for Arcadia, and becoming acquainted with Cathillian had reinforced her realization.

The Chieftain, however, had completely smashed the evil druid rumors once and for all. Ezekiel had once come to the Dark Forest asking for help in their great battle, but the Chieftain had been stern, forceful, and passionate in his refusal. Amelia hadn't been able to understand how he could have denied his old friend, the very person who had helped him discover the magic he had built an entire community on. He seemed like a disgrace, a terrible old man that she had no interest in seeing or meeting.

After having spent so much time with him in the last few days, though, she had become very aware of just how wrong she had been.

The Chieftain was a man of honor. Every move he made, he made with his people in mind. To risk fighting for Arcadia would have been to risk losing everything. If he had sent his own warriors into the fray and Adrien had won, the Chieftain was certain he would have turned his rage on the Dark Forest next.

There weren't thousands of druids, unlike the Arcadians. There were only hundreds of them, and he was certain they would all have perished if he had sent them. On top of his dedication to his tribe's safety, he spent every morning with the very young children of the forest, teaching them valuable life lessons in honor and how to grow strong plants that would survive any weather.

He spent every afternoon into the evening with the older kids —the younger teenagers—teaching them what it was to be a part of a team, a family. What it meant to be a leader, even if you didn't have the official title as he did. To him, *every* druid was a leader, and *every* druid was a prince or princess.

The Chieftain then spent every night having fun, unwinding from the day. She had seen that it was a running joke to pick on the Chieftain because he was under the impression the young people thought he was cool. The thing was, they really did.

In the Dark Forest, if someone was old enough to strike a man with a spear or an arrow, that person was old enough to drink wine with the Chieftain. He would spend his evenings until late into the night drinking wine with the young warrior recruits, teaching them about honor in battle and about respecting the enemy, but mostly about letting go.

His most important lesson was that the morning and afternoon hours should be spent training hard, but the nighttime hours were for having fun—letting go and living life the way it should be. With or without the wine, family and friends were the most important part of any community. As they got older and became actual warriors, that lesson altered slightly to "have fun whenever you aren't on duty."

Everything she had learned while growing up and even into adulthood had been wrong. Even the amazing things that Arryn had told her had been completely understated. *The Dark Forest was paradise.* It had its problems like any other place, but for the most part, it was everything she wished Arcadia could be.

Perhaps she could take these lessons back to the city with her and implement them there once everything was in place. Had Adrien only taken in what the Founder had hoped to teach him, Irth would have been quite the utopia.

The Heights, the Dark Forest, and Arcadia could all have worked together in a peaceful alliance. No one would have ever wanted for or needed anything.

But it wasn't too late.

As she headed toward the training grounds to see if she could get a few lessons in she ran into Arryn, who was no doubt traveling there for the same reason.

"Well, good morning," Amelia said. "Fancy meeting you here."

Arryn smiled. "Yeah, I had planned to be at the *Versuch* pit long before now, but I got held up by Dante."

Amelia laughed. "Let me guess... he made best friends with another tree?"

"Yes! I don't get it! Ugh. I love that baby to pieces, but he's driving me crazy. I'm about to make him some little boots so he can't climb up there anymore."

In her short time in the forest, Amelia had seen how the master-familiar bond worked. Any druid could speak with any other person's familiar, but no one would ever understand what that animal was saying better than its master or mistress.

Still, Amelia had never seen anyone quite so bonded with their familiar as Arryn was with hers. She wasn't sure if it was because it was new to her or because of her intense affinity for animals.

Arryn could speak to any animal in the forest, and she could do so with an understanding that rivaled the bond itself, even with other familiars. It made sense to Amelia that Arryn's power with animals would have intensified her bond, but still, she couldn't be certain.

With anyone else, the familiar was their companion. Their friend. A family member they would be lost without. Arryn, however, regarded the tigers as her children. Young Dante had become a son to her in such a way that she couldn't even bear to let him out of her sight most times.

It was sweet to see.

"Has he grown any since he's been here?" Amelia asked.

Arryn shook her head. "That's part of the reason why this sucks so bad. If he was bigger, I wouldn't worry so much. In the mountains, when I met them, Dante was just a tiny little thing. He wasn't much bigger than a small dog, though he was obviously a lot thicker and more muscular due to what he is. But he grew very quickly. Over a couple of days, he grew to the size of a medium-sized dog—just a little smaller than that, really. He hasn't grown an inch since."

Amelia shook her head. "That's so weird. Isn't that weird? I don't have much experience with tigers—or familiars—but it seems that Snow is way bigger than she should be."

"Snow was full-grown when I met them. The females don't usually get very big." Arryn laughed. "Well, I said that tigers don't get very big, but what I meant was that they don't get very big in comparison to what she is *now*. I didn't have any experience with tigers, but I'd seen some leopards and panthers. I didn't think there would be a huge size difference between them, but boy was I wrong. Before the growth spurt, Snow was twice the size of any leopard I had ever seen. Snow was close to three or four hundred pounds when I first saw her. During the week we spent together, she tripled in size. She must be over a thousand now. Little *baby* Dante, however, will forever be a baby, I guess."

Amelia smiled. "Yeah, but can you really complain? He's just *so* cute. He's still small enough that you can hold him in your arms and snuggle him like a baby. And he *is* a baby... As soon as he catches someone *oohing* and *aahing* over him, he sees that as an invite and jumps into their lap and demands to be loved on. He's quite the charmer, that one."

Laughing, Arryn said, "Yeah, that's no joke. He is a sweet little guy."

They walked in silence for a few moments as they headed toward the *Versuch* grounds. Amelia had been invited into Arryn's head at one point since she had been back, and the girl had allowed Amelia to see the things that she had experienced.

What she had survived, Amelia knew without a doubt she never would have. It had been one hell of a mix between skill and determination that had allowed her to thrive on that mountain.

No doubt a healthy dose of stubbornness and refusal to give up had helped as well.

"I know you've been recovering and getting more into the new mom and familiar thing the last couple days, but have you thought any more about what happens next?" Amelia asked.

Arryn huffed, her eyes darting toward Amelia's. "What is this? You're the *second* person today to suggest I've gone soft. Cathillian was the other one. Of course, I just thought he was being a dick."

"No one thinks you've gone soft," Amelia said with a smile. "We just haven't heard much about what you plan to do. I realize that I'm the Chancellor, but I also realize I can't do this without you. I wanted to let you have a couple of days to recover before I approached you."

Arryn nodded, giving a heavy sigh as her eyes wandered to the ground. "Trust me, I've been thinking a lot about it. The only thing I know for sure right now is that Scarlett *has* to die. She knows we are a threat, and she has to know that we are all tucked away in the Dark Forest. How long before she sends an army of Arcadians to our borders?"

There was a moment of silence before Amelia said, "Yes, that thought had crossed my mind as well. They could destroy this place if they wanted to. In the good old days, back before mystics were controlling everyone, everyone had a healthy respect—or fear, depending on how you wanted to look at it—of the druids of the Dark Forest. There was no way in hell an Arcadian would threaten to remove even a single *leaf* from the forest. I imagine that fear and respect will dwindle more and more everyday with Scarlett in charge."

"We need to sneak into the city and assassinate those who are closest to her. There are still several students and teachers who were in their little group I haven't killed yet. We need to remedy that."

Amelia nodded. "That sounds like a good idea. A good start,

anyway. The governor of Cella has been talking about going back to his city, just him and his son. Before he came to Arcadia, before he found out that Talia had her claws in the city, he'd made a deal with the remnant. He was supposed to deliver Talia and Scarlett to them. He never promised that he could, but he did promise information. He was supposed to meet them a week from that day. It's been four days, so he plans to go. He'll need to leave tomorrow to get there in time."

"And he seriously plans to go alone? What if they don't like his answer?" Arryn asked.

Amelia shrugged. "I don't know. I *do* know that if he doesn't show, they will rip Cella apart."

They walked a few moments in silence, and the training grounds came into view. Finally, Arryn said, "I have a feeling this war will be far worse than we imagine. It's not just Arcadia. It's the dark druids. It's the remnant. And when it comes to the city, the guards are innocent. Their minds are being twisted and manipulated on a daily basis. We are going to war with people who literally don't have a clue what they're doing."

"We have to find a way to subdue them. Lives will be lost—I'm not stupid enough to think they won't be. But we need to try to save as many as possible. Nonlethal measures, if we can pull it off."

Arryn nodded. "Sneaking into the city and pulling off some assassinations sounds better and better all the time. We should talk to the *Schatten*, the shadow warriors from the northern village. There are several here in the southern village, and I'm betting they would be more than willing to help in one way or another."

"Arryn!" Celine waved from the pit. She was there bright and early to train with Nika, as expected. She had been relentless with her training since she arrived.

"Will you be teaching or training today?" Amelia asked.

Arryn gave a dark smile. "Both. Get your ass in the pit."

Amelia's eyes widened for a moment as she realized what Arryn meant by that. "Great. Well, this should be fun."

"And painful! Don't forget painful," Arryn said with a wink.

Amelia smiled and nodded her head. "Yeah, and that. Did I tell you how glad I am to have you back?"

CHAPTER TWO

S carlett sat on the front of her desk with her legs crossed. Her red dress touched the floor, but it was slit straight up to her hip, showing off her legs as she stared down at the disheveled middle-aged man who knelt before her.

His hair was long, all different lengths, and completely unkempt. It was a dirty grey color, but she wasn't sure if that was the result of dirt or that was the actual tone. His eyes were dark blue, bordering on brown in certain light.

He was a filthy man, but Scarlett was quite certain he wasn't useless.

Her friends had circled around him like vultures, hands clasped in front of them as they stood there staring down at him. The man shook, tears rolling down his face as he waited for the new Chancellor to decide his fate. Her friends had no doubt terrified the man on the way to her office.

But that was all right. She planned to use his fear to her advantage.

"What was your name again?" Scarlett asked, her tone bored and slightly annoyed.

"H-henry, Chancellor. My name is Henry."

She pursed her lips as she nodded. "That's right... Henry. So, Henry, what brings you to my office?"

Henry nervously looked over his shoulder at the men and women behind him before wiping his tears from his face. He turned his attention back to the Chancellor, obvious confusion on his face. "Don't you already know, ma'am?"

Scarlett rolled her eyes and sighed. "Yes, Henry." She rubbed the bridge of her nose as her eyes closed. "I know exactly why you're here. What I *don't* know is your version of it. I'm interested in hearing what you have to say."

There was a pause as Henry shifted his weight from knee to knee, trying to get comfortable. His hands were bound together at the wrist, and he had pulled them tightly against his chest as if he were a child praying.

"I was caught stealing, Chancellor. My wife, she's very sick. I don't know if she'll make it, and I couldn't afford to get the supplies I needed to help her. Please, don't cut off my hands. I need them to take care of her," he begged.

Scarlett studied him, her face taut with concentration. "Well, that *is* the old way, after all. Cutting off hands, I mean. Stealing is a serious offense. If we can't trust you not to take what doesn't belong to you, how could we trust that you wouldn't use those hands to hurt the city in other ways?"

The man's eyes widened as he shook his head wildly, moving a few inches farther forward on his knees. "I would never hurt anyone. Please, you have to believe me! I would never hurt anyone. I just needed to be able to take care of my wife. I'll do anything. Anything at all. I'll help rebuild. Please, just tell me what to do, and I'll do it."

Scarlett faked a heavy sigh as she shook her head, looking the man over. "You know what my job is. You know what it entails. I have to ensure the safety of the city." She stood, making her way over to where the man knelt on the floor. "An example must be made, or the city will fall to pieces in this difficult time."

Nikolai took a step forward. "You could make an example of him, just as you suggested, but in a much different way."

Scarlett feigned interest, since this was part of the plan they had discussed in the privacy of their minds before the man had been brought to kneel at her feet.

Nikolai continued, "You are trying to build a new city. You're trying to establish yourself as a kind leader, one who understands others. If he truly was stealing to provide for his sick wife, the people would be moved by your compassion if you released him."

"Interesting. You're suggesting that we should just let him go? Or would there be stipulations to this agreement?" Scarlett asked.

"Chancellor, I would suggest allowing him to clean himself. Give him something other than rags to wear. Provide the supplies his wife requires to live, and allow this man the opportunity to continue to walk the streets so the people see just how kind you truly are." Nikolai gave her a wink and a knowing smile.

Henry suddenly became very motivated and excited. He nodded his head, his eyes wide as he flattened his hands against one another in a praying fashion. "Yes! Please! I promise you that I'll do just that. I'll tell everyone of your kindness. I'm from the Boulevard, and our people stick together. If you give my wife this chance to live by giving me this opportunity, I'll work hard to make sure everyone sees what I see. Someone worth following. Someone truly just and compassionate."

Scarlett held her look of concentration for a few moments before slowly breaking into a smile. Finally, she nodded. "Henry, today's a new day. I'm so happy we found a solution that doesn't require bloodshed or you being forced into a cell away from your wife. There are plenty of empty noble houses. There is no reason for you to live in squalor. I'll have some guards help you move your wife to one of those homes. You clean yourself up, get her well, and we will call on you when we need you."

Tears filled the man's eyes as he leaned forward and kissed the floor directly in front of her. "Thank you! Thank you so much.

You have no idea how you have helped my family. You won't regret this, I promise."

Scarlett stood, nodding her head toward the door. "Oh, you're quite welcome, Henry. And believe me, I won't."

Henry was led out of the building by Vanessa and Theo, who unbound his wrists and spoke to him with feather-light voices. It was only one person, of course, but that one person would go a long way to securing her seat. She had no true claim to the office of Chancellor, so anyone could challenge her at any moment. It would be little actions like this that would keep her self-proclaimed position safe.

Barbara stepped forward with a smile on her face. Her eyes were green and shaped like a cat's, and the very color complemented her dark skin and red-painted lips. She had long medium-blonde hair that hung in a loose braid over her shoulder, with curly tendrils escaping around her hairline.

"Everything seems to be off to a good start. Shall we keep searching for degenerates?" she asked.

"Absolutely. I plan to use good old Henry as my champion. He will walk the streets and praise me to anyone he can get to listen. Shouldn't be too difficult, at least with those Boulevard shits. The more names we add to the list of people who worship the ground we walk on, the better off we'll be."

Barbara smiled. "That shouldn't be too difficult. The weak-minded are always eager to please. The city is full of followers. We should have an easy go of it. Where should we start?"

Scarlett walked around her desk and took a seat in the over-stuffed chair. "Start with the barracks. That will be the most important. Once we have the support of the Guard, we will have the support of the people. Do it while they're sleeping. Anyone is an easy target while sleeping. It shouldn't even take very much magic on your part to plant a few suggestive thoughts."

Nikolai smiled. "As you wish. This will be fun."

Scarlett gave her own wicked smile. "Oh, sweetheart, you

have no idea. Once we have the Guard in the palms of our hands, we have every tool necessary to rip apart our enemies. The first thing I plan to do once our position is secured is move on the Dark Forest. I plan to burn the bitch to the ground."

WHILE EVERYONE else was at the training pit or clinging to the Chieftain's every word, Samuel snuck off and made his way down to the river. The Kalt River was not only beautiful, it was peaceful and quiet. It was also where he had initially met the druids.

Arryn and Elysia had found him after he passed out and collapsed in the river. He had washed downstream, and was nearly dead in the cold water when they came upon him.

After they pulled him out, they had healed him. He hadn't trusted them or their magic at the time, but he had quickly come around. Samuel, being a rearick, had a natural distrust for any form of magic. His people didn't believe in it, so none of them had ever practiced it—at least as far as Samuel knew.

He nearly laughed as he pulled the seeds from his pocket and held them in his hand. He studied them, taking a deep breath and letting it out as he wondered if he should be doing this.

Not long before—though it seemed like a lifetime now— Samuel and a man named Andrew had saved a group of loggers close to the border of the Madlands. Miraculously, no one had died, but several had been injured, and some of those injuries would have festered and killed them later had it not been for the arrival of Arryn and her friend, Cathillian.

Cathillian had healed the men and taken them under his wing. He had taken it upon himself to escort them outside the city walls every day and taught them nature magic. Taught them how to grow trees to replace the ones they cut down. He had hoped to teach them even more, like healing, so they might never have to fear for their lives again.

Out of all the students, there had only been a couple who had a true underlying talent. An affinity for nature magic.

And Samuel had been one of them.

He had sworn off it, vowing that he would never learn such a thing. He hadn't seen the point of it—until Celine was nearly killed during a dark druid invasion.

He had held the girl in his arms, watching her bleed out. There was nothing he could do to save her, and he relived the terror he had gone through when he had found out his own family had been killed.

He had grown very fond of the young woman in the short time he had known her, and the thought of losing her completely devastated him. Somehow, he had found the strength to heal her in the midst of all that.

The power came bursting out of him in his most desperate moment, and he had saved her life. It was because of that moment that he decided he would never take such a risk again.

Now, he had a new vow. *He would never risk her life again.*

Samuel laid the seeds on the ground in front of him. He had found them just outside the Chieftain's hut. They were kept in little bags, and he had seen the kids take them in the mornings before class. The kids would each grab a bag out of the basket and head off with the Chieftain.

He wasn't sure what type of seeds they were, but he hoped that with practice he would be able to figure that out once it grew and bloomed.

Samuel hadn't actually tried any of the things he had seen Cathillian teaching the other students when they were still in Arcadia, but he had listened to his words, paid attention to the lessons. Now, he wondered if a part of him might have known that he would end up where he was, with the necessity to learn.

After drilling a small hole in the damp ground with his finger,

Samuel put one of the seeds in and packed the dirt around it. He set the little bag to the side and leaned forward, laying his hands flat on the ground on either side.

He took a deep breath and exhaled heavily, then closed his eyes and focused hard on the seed he planted. After a moment, Samuel felt warm. His entire body heated up, but he mainly felt it in his hands. He remembered Cathillian instructing the others to push the heat into the ground, so he did. There was no way for him to know if what he was doing was correct, but he was determined to get it right one way or another.

"Imagine the heat in your body as a stream of water."

Samuel jumped when he heard the voice behind him. He turned to see the Chieftain standing there, a knowing smile on his face.

"I dunno what yer talkin' about," Samuel said, bringing his knee up and preparing to stand.

"No, no," the Chieftain requested. "Don't get up yet. You were doing well, but you need a little direction."

Samuel shook his head, embarrassment filling him. He had wanted to do this alone; he didn't want anyone else to know. "Eh, this is all a buncha crazy anyway. My people hate magic. It can make a man do terrible things, and we don't see no reason to use it anyway. All we need's our two perfectly good hands, a strong back, and a good axe or hammer."

Samuel looked up and saw the Chieftain smiling down at him. "Only a man with darkness in his heart will do terrible things. You are as pure-hearted as they come, Samuel. You're not here for power. You're here because you managed to save the life of a young lady, and it was only by chance. Luck. That's it. You're here because you're not sure you will get that lucky again."

Samuel's brows furrowed as he searched the Chieftain's eyes. His words stung Samuel, but he couldn't deny their truth. What if he *didn't* get that lucky again? What if he couldn't figure out how it worked and next time she actually died?

They were about to head into a battle, and he knew Celine wouldn't take no for an answer. He knew there was no chance of her staying behind where it was safe in the Forest.

"Ye know how my people are, and why I wouldn't want this known. I came here ta be alone. I remember the things Cathillian taught the others. I hoped I could figure it out on me own. I don't want anyone ta know, because I don't want anyone ta know if I fail."

The Chieftain took a step forward, his staff touching the ground. "You won't fail. If you can call on that much magic in the heat of the moment, you have a lot to offer. I'll make you a deal— if you let me give you a lesson, I'll keep my mouth shut." The Chieftain smiled deviously. "If not, well, I won't say I can be trusted, especially if I have a little bit of that wine. I make the *best* wine, you know. It's *strong*. Affects a man's ability to keep a secret if he doesn't have motivation."

Samuel shook his head. "Ye really do have the mind of a kid, don't ye? Unbelievable."

The Chieftain shrugged. "Well, I do have a reputation to uphold. Besides, you're right: I *do* know your people. I'm curious to see what you can do."

With a heavy sigh, Samuel nodded. "Fine. But I swear, if ye say a word…"

The Chieftain laughed. "Trust me, I have no intention of feeling the wrath of that hammer of yours. Now, you had all the fundamentals right. Kneel, place your hands on either side of the seed, and then close your eyes and focus."

Samuel turned and did as he was told, kneeling and placing his hands on the ground. He closed his eyes and tried to repeat what he had done earlier, and soon Samuel felt the heat in his body rise again. It reminded him of what it felt like to be in the warm, spring sun when the air was still crisp.

The Chieftain stepped forward. "Now, imagine that the heat flowing through you is a stream of water. Your body is full of trenches. Focus on the water and will it to flow through your body. Move it down from your mind, through your shoulders, down through your arms, and out your fingertips."

Thinking of the power flowing through him as something tangible and as familiar to him as water somehow made it easier for him to connect to the magic. He imagined a shallow stream of water pouring from his brain and making its way through his body to flow out through his fingers.

Before long, he felt the heat passing into his hands and moving into the ground, and for a moment, he could sense the seed in the ground. He felt it break, and then he felt the life blooming within the dirt.

Samuel risked a peek and saw a green stem sprouting from the ground with a small bud on top that had yet to open. There were several leaves stretching from the side of the stem.

Lilies. The seeds had been lily seeds.

"*Shite*! I did it!" Samuel exclaimed, total shock on his face.

The Chieftain smiled, walking around and kneeling in front of Samuel. "Rearick, there is life waiting inside of you. In fact, that is true in more ways than one."

Samuel wondered if he was talking about Celine right then. "I'll take yer word fer it, old man."

"Well, *young man*, it seems to me that you *are* gifted. Now you know how to grow a plant. But I suspect you were out to learn something different, yes?"

Samuel stared at the lily bud for a moment before turning his gaze back to the Chieftain and nodding. "I wanna learn how ta heal. It has come ta me attention that it might be a good skill ta have."

The corner of the Chieftain's mouth turned up, obviously knowing what had changed his mind. "Shall we make another deal?"

Samuel narrowed his eyes as he thought over the Chieftain's proposal. Finally, he said, "Depends on what it is."

The Chieftain stood and pointed to an area a bit closer to the tree line, where the grass was thickest. "That bit right there has the richest soil. You can tell because the blades of grass are thicker and greener than anywhere else. I would say that would be quite a nice place to plant a flower garden. In fact, I'd have to say that if someone were inclined to plant a garden there, I might be willing to give them private lessons and keep my mouth shut about it. After all, even with all its many shades, the Forest can always use a bit more color."

Samuel stared at the wide-open space for a few moments before turning back to the Chieftain. "And if a man were ta do such a thing, how soon would 'e have ta have it done? And what kinda private lessons would be involved?"

"I think two days' time is more than plenty for any nature magic user with promise, and if he can grow flowers with beautiful blooms, I would have to say the next logical step would be healing. The power to create is always the first step. It teaches respect for life and the true cost of a life lost, even for something that others may deem insignificant like a tree or a rose. Once a man can create, he can learn how to heal."

The Chieftain took a few steps forward, his expression almost excited. As he passed Samuel, he clapped him on the back. "Two days, rearick. Let's see what this hypothetical person can do."

Samuel sighed heavily, the weight of the challenge settling on him. He stared down at the flower he had created; a tiny little thing, but new life nonetheless. "Bitch and Bastard. Yeah, let's see, old man."

CHAPTER THREE

The governor of Cella finished packing up his things and readying his horse, with Nathaniel not far behind. Arryn and Amelia both stood and watched, their arms crossed and worry in their expressions. Neither of them believed the governor should go back to Cella on his own to meet the remnant leader, but he was determined.

If he didn't go, he feared the worst for Cella. The entire city had been abandoned. Not a single person, young or old, had been left behind. Even the sick and the dying had been relocated, placed on bedding inside carts and tended to by doctors all the way to Arcadia to ensure their comfort.

When he had discussed it with Amelia before, the governor had been overcome with emotion, hoping for the best for those people that had been left in Arcadia while he and the Guard fled.

He had felt like a coward, leaving the people who had come to depend on him most, but maybe they wouldn't believe that of him.

He hoped they thought he was on his way back to Cella to defend it. The idea that his people might see him as a coward deflated his sense of purpose, but Arryn and Amelia had both assured him that he had done the right thing.

Had he stayed in Arcadia with his people, he would have run the risk of his own Guard being compelled by mystical magic to do things they wouldn't normally do—like attack innocent people.

Amelia had told him that his presence would have been wasted there, because he nor his Guard would have been allowed to keep their free will.

With the Cellan Guard, had they remained in Arcadia, they would have been tasked with training the Arcadian Guard and improving their skills. With that number of experienced fighters, it would have made it nearly impossible for Arryn to go in and expect to win.

Slowly, he came around to see what everyone else already had —that he couldn't protect anyone if he got killed before the fight even began—but the meeting with the remnant leader was non-negotiable. He wouldn't allow his vacant city to be torn to pieces because he was too afraid to hold up his end of the deal.

"Are you sure we can't come with you?" Arryn asked.

Nathaniel walked over and threw an extra blanket over the back of his father's horse, then turned to Arryn and smiled. "We appreciate the offer, but this is something we have to do alone. The remnant leader expects that, and to bring backup—well, I think it would look like we were going to let them down."

Arryn smiled and shook her head. "I admire the bravery, and I understand the reasoning, but I still feel like this could go badly. *We* can't afford to lose you any more than your people can. You will play an important role in what we plan to do. Besides, do you honestly think he'll show up alone?"

Nathaniel sighed, thinking about her words. He took a step forward, leaving barely any room between them, and Arryn swallowed hard as she looked up into his eyes.

"What if we agree to take three warriors with us? Will that make you feel better?" he asked, smiling.

The governor turned. "Is that wise, son?"

Nathaniel turned to his father. "She's right. Do we really expect the remnant leader to show up without backup? They're always prepared for battle. *Always*. While I think we need to take as few people as possible, I also agree with Arryn that going alone would be a terrible idea. She's made some really good points."

The governor gave a small smile and nodded. "I suppose you're right. I'm glad I have you around, son. I think too much with my heart, not enough with my head. Being a compassionate leader is nothing to be ashamed of, but in situations like this, situations I've been lucky enough never to be put in before, I tend to go more with what *feels* right then what *is* right. Still, I couldn't help but notice you said 'warriors.' Not Guard?"

Amelia nodded, speaking up then. "Warriors are a much better idea. I think everyone here would agree."

The governor shook his head. "Why wouldn't I take my own men? They represent the city we mean to save."

"I mean no offense, Governor," Arryn began, "but a single druid warrior can fight like ten of your men. They're worth twenty of the Arcadian guardsman. These men and women have been training since before they would be considered old enough to attend the Academy. When they can hold a spear, they start training, which is a far more rigorous and painful way to learn than any single guard in Cella or Arcadia could even dream of. If you want to take fewer men, you need to take druid warriors."

"Not only that," Elysia said as she walked up and joined the group, "but I'm sure that if you asked nicely, the Elders would be more than happy to oblige."

She winked and smiled. "Besides, we have a lot of your men, so it's a fair trade. And if you want to have any chance of getting away, physical magic is *not* going to save you. If they bring enough men, you won't have the strength to create enough fireballs to stop them. But vines, thorns, powerful winds... Those are things that can slow an enemy down long enough to get you to safety."

The governor sighed, nodding as a smile crossed his face. "Point taken. The more you talk about your warriors, the more I realize exactly why the men and women of the Arcadian Valley fear you. It also makes me realize that we are *severely* under-trained in comparison, and I can assure you my men are very deadly as is."

Elysia laughed. "Thank you for the compliment, Governor. I'm sure your men are extremely effective, but as Arryn said before, we start early, and we start hard. If you so much as raised your hand to a ten-year-old in this village, you'd be taken to the ground in a matter of seconds. Perhaps when this is all said and done, we can give you some tips. It might keep you from getting into a situation like this again."

The governor's face grew serious, his brows furrowing as he considered her offer, and finally, he nodded. "That would be a debt I could never repay. Thank you! And thank you for the warriors, if you're actually offering."

She smiled. "Absolutely. It seems that in Arryn's travels, she's managed to reunite the people of the valley. Our lives are at risk, just as yours are. You've offered to help us, so it's our turn to return the favor."

Within moments, three warriors walked their horses over to the group. They bowed their heads, placing their hands over their hearts. Elysia returned the salute.

"Ryel, keep back. Don't get too close once they reach Cella. Just watch for any kind of hostility or quick action. If anyone engages, take them down. If there are too many, focus on getting the governor and his son to safety. Evasion tactics, understood?" Elysia said.

Ryel nodded. "Yes, Elysia. Understood."

The warriors once again saluted before getting on their

horses. Nathaniel and the governor mounted as well.

The governor looked down at Elysia and Arryn. "Thank you both. I know we're both stubborn men, but we just want what's best for our people. We'll do whatever it takes to ensure their safety."

Arryn smiled. "Trust me, I can understand that. I have two homes, not one, and it looks like as soon as the battle to free Arcadia—again—is done, there will be another battle here in the Dark Forest. I know what it means to feel responsible for the lives of others. Never apologize for that, and never be afraid to accept help either. I need it quite often."

Nathaniel sighed as he smiled down at Arryn. "Beautiful and deadly. I don't think it would be possible to have a more dangerous combination."

Arryn's eyes widened for a moment, silence quickly finding her. She obviously had no idea how to respond to such a statement.

Elysia cleared her throat. "Safe travels, gentlemen!"

She smiled and waved before turning and grabbing Arryn's hand, pulling her away.

The governor and his son urged their horses forward, and after several yards' distance had been placed between them and the women of the Dark Forest, the governor turned to his son. "What the hell was that?"

Nathaniel's eyes widened as he shrugged his shoulders. "I don't know. It just slipped out!"

"Slipped out? Are you *trying* to get the crap kicked out of us?" the governor asked, an exasperated smile on his face as he shook his head. "Damn, son! Show some subtlety and some restraint."

Nathaniel laughed. "I'm sorry, I couldn't help it. Can you blame me? You've heard the stories. You've seen her. A woman like that doesn't come around very often. She got me a little worried about not coming back, so I felt compelled to say something."

There was laughter behind them. Nathaniel looked over his shoulder with a smile on his face. "Hey, are you making fun of me back there?"

One of the warriors shook her head with an amused expression. She was a beautiful, dark-skinned woman with long, dark hair. Her multiple braids had been plaited into a much larger, single braid that hung down her back. "Feel compelled all you like, impatient one. She certainly is beautiful, and she's come a long way since she first stepped foot in the Dark Forest. But if you plan to pursue that one... Well, I think you're going to have quite the fight on your hands."

Nathaniel sighed and shook his head. "Damn. So, she's spoken for? The last thing I want to do is piss off a druid, but I can't deny that it would be worth it."

The governor laughed. "Son, you're young. You think a woman like that would be unattached?"

Nathaniel shrugged. "I can hope, can't I?" He turned back to the warrior, who was still laughing at him. "What's your name?"

"My name is Cassondra. The warrior to my left is Ryel, and the warrior to my right is Clara."

"Well, Cassondra, at the risk of dashing a young man's dreams, are you laughing at me because she's spoken for, or are you laughing at me because I stand no chance?" Nathaniel asked.

"I laugh because of both. She's alone, but there is another who's had his eyes on her since they were very young. If she chose another man, he would support her, but he sure as hell wouldn't be happy about it. However, at the risk of crushing your dreams, I assure you, the other man she might one day choose would not be you." She laughed again.

Shaking his head, Nathaniel said, "Man, I'm starting to think we should have gone by ourselves."

The governor laughed. "Why, son? I would've missed out on all this entertainment."

CHAPTER FOUR

E lysia, feeling Arryn's discomfort with Nathaniel's compliments, grabbed her hand to usher her away. Once there was plenty of distance between them, Elysia began laughing. "What the *hell* was that?"

Arryn shrugged, her eyes wide. "I don't know! I've barely talked to the guy. He seems nice. Actually, more than nice. He's intelligent, seems like a dedicated son, and he's definitely loyal to his people—but no. Absolutely not, so you can wipe that look off your face."

Arryn rolled her eyes. "I don't have time for anything like that. Besides, I doubt very seriously there's a man on earth who can deal with my bad attitude. I mean, have you heard the terrible things I say to Cathillian? And he's my best friend!"

Elysia shook her head. "There will come a time when the interest will be there. Especially in the Dark Forest. From what I've been told, you Arcadians are much more... *prudish* than we are. We don't share the idea that a marriage is required to pursue happiness with someone. Once the battles are fought, and your job is done, you might find yourself looking for your next adventure."

"I appreciate the sentiment, but if you're preparing to give me 'the life talk,' that ship has sailed for Cathillian and me both."

Silence filled the air as Elysia looked at Arryn in shock. "What? And neither one of you said anything?"

A look of confusion crossed Arryn's face. "You can't be serious. You think he's a virgin? Cathillian is the most ridiculous flirt I've ever seen in my entire life."

Elysia's eyes narrowed. "Are we talking about the same thing? Did you not mean that you and Cathillian…"

Realization struck Arryn and her eyes widened as she gasped, waving her hands in the air. "No! Dear Goddess. Hell no! I just meant that neither of us is in need of *the talk*. Cathillian and I have *never ever* considered anything like that. *Ever*." She gave a shocked and exasperated sigh, shaking her head. "Never."

Elysia laughed, releasing a relieved breath of her own. "Well, that was awkward. As for my son, I was more than aware of Cathillian's little *adventures* long ago. It was hard to ignore the girls, all sitting in circles pointing and giggling, only to turn around and act all shy around him. You, however, I didn't realize. I suppose you've been a woman for a while, and I had no idea. Just one more thing I allowed to go unnoticed."

Arryn shook her head as they continued to walk. "I didn't want anyone to know about it. I threatened to burn his balls off if he ever told anyone, and he promised he wouldn't. He also said he didn't know who he was more afraid of, me or Cathillian, so that was a good motivator for him. Shockingly enough, he was honest and never did say anything."

That brought another smile to Elysia's face. "I'd like to say I was surprised, but I'm not. Who was it? I have to know."

Arryn burst into a fit of laughter. "It was funny then, because he was kind of goofy. But he filled out quite a bit once he began warrior training, even if he did start late."

With a gasp and wide eyes, Elysia asked, "Really? Mason?"

Arryn nodded.

"Oh, my," Elysia said. "Don't tell my son—he'd break his neck. He's always thought Mason had a thing for you, and he's always hated him."

With confusion on her face, Arryn asked, "Why would he have a problem with it? It's none of his business, just like all the royal druid groupies sliming their way around him weren't any of mine."

"Royal druid groupies?" Elysia snorted as she shook her head. "You may be grown now, and you may be capable of great things, but you still have a lot to learn. Apparently, you're just as blind in some areas as I've been."

Arryn opened her mouth to speak, but closed it when footsteps approached. They looked behind them to see Amelia approaching.

"I wanted to see them off," Amelia said, completely oblivious to the serious conversation that had just been taking place. "So, what now?"

With a sigh, Arryn shrugged. "This is the hard part. Personally, I feel like this is the calm before the storm. The dark druids have been quiet, and we have yet to hear anything from Arcadia. But like them, we're just sitting here doing nothing. The question is, who's going to move first? Obviously, it needs to be us."

"We have scouts due back sometime today," Elysia said. "They should have news of the dark druids. Hopefully, soon. Once we know what they're up to, we can begin planning. As for Arcadia, we have no idea yet what they're capable of."

Amelia shook her head. "That's not entirely true. I know what they're capable of. I've seen what a strong mystic can do. Julianne, the Master of the mystics, infiltrated the Guard during the Battle for Arcadia. She spent weeks disguised as another person. Weeks forcing other people to see what she wanted them to see. All day. All night. Dozens of people—or more—at a time. They even sent her to the Frozen North with a group. I'm pretty sure Arryn could attest to how difficult it is to focus in that kind of weather."

"Fuck me," Arryn said. "I can't even imagine. It took me weeks to gain enough strength to get off that mountain. I was bled out before I was dumped there, but still! The ability it must've taken her to hold an illusion for that long... She must be *very* strong. But as Amelia was trying to say, that just goes to show how powerful she was. Imagine what a mystic in *comfortable* conditions could do."

"Not just her, either. By now, I'm sure she has friends there. Before everything started to get really bad, Julianne stopped to tell me there was a group of mystics called the 'New Dawn' that was in the area, and was very dangerous. I told her about our own little problem, and though she didn't know if Scarlett was part of New Dawn, she did realize the woman was quite a threat.

"Whether or not she's part of it, there are others like Scarlett out there. Mystics who left the temple early, or trained on their own. She's got to know Arryn's coming for her. There's no way in hell she's going to try to keep that city under control all by herself."

Silence filled the air for a few moments as the three women thought over their situation. Finally, Arryn said, "Do you think Julianne would help Arcadia again?"

Amelia's expression turned to sadness. "I have no doubt about that. Julianne would be by our sides in an instant if she could. But like I said, she's dealing with the New Dawn. She has problems of her own to solve. As far as I know, she's not in the Temple, but that doesn't mean someone else wouldn't be willing to help."

"Are you suggesting we go to the Temple of the Mystics?" Elysia asked.

Arryn's face lit up. "Why not? If Scarlett has friends, why shouldn't we make some, too? We need information on how to beat them. Who better to go to than the people of the Temple? The closest thing we have to a mystic is Amelia."

She turned to the Chancellor. "No offense, but you're not that skilled. You can get into the minds of others, but that's it."

"I hate that I can't make these journeys with you," Elysia said, shaking her head. "If the threat of war with the dark druids weren't pressing down on us, I would go with you in a heartbeat."

Arryn smiled. "Trust me, I know that. But this is something we'll have to do if we're going to have a chance to beat her."

Amelia nodded. "I'll go tell the others. It's going to take all of us to make that trip, and we should go soon. Besides, it'll probably do Samuel some good to be back home in Craigston for a while."

Elysia followed, but kept a safe distance behind Arryn and Amelia. Though she had known the time for them to leave again was coming soon, she had hoped it would have been a while longer.

ALARIC STEPPED outside the cave that sat at the southernmost edge of the Dark Forest. The sun shone from above, but it did nothing to brighten the gloom in the area. The trees had almost no foliage, and the leaves that still existed looked ashy or had turned brown, ready to fall at any moment.

Spring was in full bloom everywhere else in the Valley, but not here. The bark on the mighty oaks looked as though it had been burned, charred, or simply smoked slowly and steadily over time. Few were still alive, and the living ones only hung on by a thread.

There were no animals. Birds had stopped singing long ago, the deer had moved farther north, and all other wildlife had dispersed right along with them. With no grass, no berries—no vegetation at all aside from the rot the dark druids were able to conjure with their tainted magic—the rabbits, raccoons, birds, and even snakes had all fled. Each species had been aware that death would find them, either from starvation or the hands of the dark druids dwelling in those woods.

But it wouldn't be like this forever—not if Alaric had anything to say about it.

He stepped farther away from the mouth of the cave, reaching his long arms into the sky and leaning back in a deep stretch. His people loitered around the area, some of them prepping what few edibles they could grow while others sparred with one another.

Running his fingers through his long, dark hair, he sighed. Something had to be done. Too many of his people had been killed. Several had been lost when they had gone to retrieve Jenna, Amara, and Flynn, the family of his most trusted confidant, Aeris.

Far more than he would have wanted to sacrifice, but he knew if she was half as strong as her brother, she was a worthy cause.

And from what he had seen, she showed great promise.

The parents seemed to be rather docile, but he didn't mind. That just meant they weren't the rebellious type. They were there to be with their children, and that was all that mattered to him. It would keep them in line.

For the time being, Jenna spent all her time training their fighters and, most importantly, she stayed out of his way. Aeris was the only one he allowed to be around him for any length of time, and that was how he liked it. He kept the number of people he trusted low to avoid problems.

The dark chieftain looked like anyone else in his charge, but was so much different. The hair that hung in long, straight, thick strands most of the way down his back had once been black. Before he had left the northern tribes, the true druids of the Dark Forest, his hair had been blacker than the darkest night.

Now, it was the color of ash. There were silver streaks throughout, but almost all of it was the deep color of burnt charcoal. His irises were terrifying, the very outer edges rimmed in black while the centers varied between the same color as his hair and a very light green. They gave him a ghostly appearance, when paired with his dark-greyish skin.

No one else in the tribe matched his appearance—he was an original, or so it seemed. He looked as if he had been born that way, but that hadn't been the case at all. He had been a beautiful baby with vibrant green eyes, medium-complected skin, and satiny black hair.

As he grew older, his looks only intensified. Once he began training under the Chieftain of the Dark Forest, his naturally green eyes intensified, his skin became even healthier, and his hair even more beautiful. He had been affected by the nature magic, just as the rest of them had been.

The women of the tribe wanted him, and many of the men in the tribe were jealous of him. He had stolen quite a few hearts, taking those women right out of the arms of other men. For Alaric, it had been quite easy.

But all that had changed when he had abandoned the Chieftain and their way of life and gone out on his own. Though his looks hadn't withered like those of many others in his tribe had over the years, he had certainly become a different type of beautiful. Dark, alluring, and terrifying.

The dark chieftain caught movement out of the corner of his eye, and he turned to see Aeris making his way over. "Not this early," Alaric said. "That's worry I see on your face. You know I don't like to see that, especially this early in the morning."

Aeris had the good sense to stop and avert his eyes for a moment, collecting himself before turning his gaze back to the dark chieftain. "Forgive me. It's just... I've been thinking. We need men. Experienced men. We need help."

Alaric laughed. "You think I don't know this? We had small numbers to begin with. Unlike the druids of the Dark Forest, we aren't elitists—we accept outsiders. We could recruit, but it would take too long. We've lost far too many people already, and it was all in the name of *testing* things."

Once again, Aeris lowered his head, gently nodding in obvious submission. "I know—those were my fault. It's just, I wanted us to know what we would be up against before we launched an actual attack. Had we gone all-in, the outcome would've been no different. While we lost a lot of people in the process, at least now we know that we need even more than we had originally to win."

The dark chieftain sighed. "I contemplated gutting you myself, but I just couldn't bring myself to do it. You're the closest thing I have to a son."

Aeris' brows creased. "But, Chieftain, you have many sons."

The corner of the dark chieftain's mouth turned up. "Have you met them? They're idiots. All of them. My daughters, too. If I'm quite honest with myself, I don't know how they've survived this long. As I said, you're the closest thing I have to a son."

Aeris smiled, his eyes lighting up with obvious pride. "That's an honor, sir. Thank you. I promise I won't let you down again."

Giving a curt nod, Alaric said, "Good. See that you don't. While I hold more patience for you than for my biological children, I can't exactly tell you how far that goes. If we lose more men—by which I mean, if I lose any chance of gaining the Dark Forest—I can't guarantee your safety. Is that understood?"

Eyes widening, Aeris nodded quickly. "Yes, of course."

"So, what's all this you wanted to talk to me about? From the earlier inflection in your voice, I assume you have a solution in mind. Is that so?"

"I don't know. I may have. There are other tribes, aren't there? Didn't you once tell me that your brother has a tribe west of here? In the Terres Forest?"

There was a pause before the dark chieftain nodded. "I did. Are you suggesting what I think you are?"

Aeris hesitated before continuing. "I am. I don't know your situation, but considering I've not seen your brother in the decade I've known you and you've never gone to see him, I have no choice but to assume the two of you don't get along. That being said, I can't imagine he would want his brother to get killed."

A dark smile spread across Alaric's face. "Jerick has always been… competitive. He was also a spoiled brat. However, despite our differences, I would have to agree. I certainly wouldn't want to see him dead. If he asked for my aid, I'd give it. I can't speak for him, but I'd hope he'd feel same."

Aeris risked a smile. "Maybe we should give him a chance. We don't have the numbers to attack the Dark Forest again. We don't even have the numbers to send scouts. I came because I have reports their scouts are hiding in the trees just at the edge of their border, where the leaves will still hide them. Right now, the only thing stopping them from coming over is thinking we have the numbers to take them. If they get brave, they'll know within minutes that we don't. I think we should abandon our post here and head west. Come back with an army."

The dark chieftain looked around, watching his people move through their camp. They had no more than fifty—seventy-five at best. There was no way an army that small could defend against the druids of the Dark Forest. It would be a massacre.

After a few moments, the dark chieftain nodded. "Gather your things. Spread the word for everyone else to do the same. We leave for the Terres Forest tonight."

CHAPTER FIVE

The sun had set on the Dark Forest, and training had been concluded for the evening. Everyone scattered to their dwellings to ready themselves for the evening festivities. Every night, after training was through, everyone gathered for wine and laughter.

The most responsible of them would only have a single cup, maybe two, but others enjoyed the wine a little too much.

But even amid the fun and relaxation, there were warriors placed all over, watching the borders and remaining on alert for any sign of magic or humans approaching.

Arryn sighed heavily, wiping sweat from her forehead with her arm as she threw the bow Elysia had crafted from a limb of the *Heilig* tree over her shoulder and walked back to her house.

Future plans had been weighing on her all that day, leaving her unsure of what would happen. She worried about the governor, and she even worried about his son Nathaniel—who apparently had a crush on her.

She smiled, shaking her head as she thought about how forward he had been. It wasn't the first time she had been flirted with, but it had certainly been one of the most entertaining times.

As Arryn walked onto the bare ground that was the foundation of many druid dwellings, she yawned and rubbed her sore arms.

Not only had she trained with Nika and Elysia, but she had also helped train Amelia, Celine, and Maddie. All three of them were quick learners and excellent students, but that hadn't made today any less physically taxing.

Maddie enjoyed attending the Chieftain's classes, though she mainly listened to him teach the children. She tried to help him keep them focused, which seemed to make her feel content and useful in the Forest.

Later in the day, when the more advanced classes began, she would come to the pit and watch Arryn and the others spar, joining in to learn some fighting techniques as well.

Amelia and Celine, however, had taken to physical training much like Arryn had when she first began. Celine's motivations were purely based on her need to protect her family, while Amelia wanted to continue to hone her skills to always be prepared for the worst. She was in charge of an entire city after all, or at least, she would be again soon.

Just before she was about to walk into her house, she heard a very pathetic—but adorable—attempt at a loud growl. She looked up just in time to see Dante leap from the roof, and he quickly took her to the ground.

She landed hard, which hurt her aching muscles, but she quickly found herself laughing as the cub violently headbutted her and rubbed his cheeks against hers, loud purrs coming from deep in his little chest.

She heard louder purrs of contentment and looked over to see Snow stalking between her house and another one. The large tiger flopped down on the ground next to Arryn, laying her massive head on Arryn's stomach and throwing a giant paw over her excited cub to calm him.

Until that moment, lying in the dirt, smothered in the warmth of the two creatures most important to her in the world, Arryn hadn't realized just how tired she was.

Running the fingers of one hand along Snow's powerful jaw while the other hand stroked Dante's back, she found her eyes growing heavy. It didn't matter that she was lying on the ground; she had been in far worse places. Her eyes fluttered closed for a moment before the call of a hawk echoed above.

Arryn gasped, jumping as her eyes snapped open. She realized that she had fallen asleep, even if it had only been for a few moments. She looked at the hawk staring down at her from the peak of her house.

"What is it, Shae?" Arryn asked, recognizing the familiar of one of the warriors who had been sent south on a scouting mission.

Arryn took a deep breath, summoning what little strength she had left. Her eyes flashed green as she magically reached out to the raptor. She was flooded with images of the dark druids making their way west. They had all their belongings on their backs, so it was obvious they weren't headed to war.

But what *were* they doing?

She wondered if maybe they were headed toward a better patch of forest, one that had more vegetation that hadn't been turned to rot with their dark magic.

"Are they migrating? Or traveling?"

More images flashed, only this time it was of Shae's master, Killian, telling her what to do.

"Find Arryn or any of the Elders. Tell them the dark druids are heading toward the Terres Forest. They're traveling under the cover of darkness."

The Terres Forest.

That lay just to the west of the Dark Forest. What could possibly be there?

Arryn shuffled out from under her tigers and dusted herself off. "Get back to Killian, Shae. I'll tell the others. Thank you." Arryn was so tired that she actually saluted the hawk, placing her fist over her heart. She shook her head, realizing what she had done, though it wasn't as if it had been a terrible mistake.

Snow rubbed against Arryn and she looked over to see the tiger's crystalline blue eyes staring hard into hers. Without speaking, she knew Snow was offering to carry her anywhere she needed to go.

With a sigh of relief, Arryn nodded and climbed on her back, leaning forward and wrapping her arms around the big cat as they made their way toward the gathering.

"Damn, you look like shit," Cathillian said, a smile on his face as he helped Arryn down.

"You know, if I could just subsist entirely on your compliments, my life would be complete. Really."

Cathillian laughed. "Well, you know. I'm always here to help. So, what's up?" As he spoke those last words, he allowed his fingers to linger on her arms, his eyes glowing for a moment as he pushed magic through her to heal her intense fatigue. Within moments, she blinked her eyes several times, enjoying the feeling of being more refreshed. Already, the muscle aches were gone, and she was more herself.

"Thanks," she said. "I guess you're not *always* a turd. Anyway, Shae just flew in. Killian sent her ahead because the dark druids are on the move."

Cathillian's face turned serious then. "On the move? Where to?"

Arryn raised her hands a bit, signaling for him to calm himself. "Relax. According to Killian, they're going toward the Terres Forest. From the images I saw, they had all their belongings with them. They're going there for a purpose, not just simple travel."

Cathillian exhaled in relief and nodded. "That seems like an unlikely thing to happen."

Just then, the Chieftain walked up, a large smile on his face and a cup of wine in each hand. "Arryn, you made it! I was worried. I heard how much you trained today."

Arryn smiled. "Yeah, but I kicked their asses."

Laughing, the Chieftain said, "You should take it easy. You've been constantly working since you've been back. Nonstop training. There *are* others who can help, you know."

Damn, did she know it! Still, she couldn't bring herself to just sit back and watch others do the work. More than ever before, she was a part of the Dark Forest. Arcadia had always held a place in her heart, but she had realized in her journeys that it would never be *home* again. Not truly, anyway.

Arryn pointed toward the cups of wine the Chieftain held. "I appreciate the sentiment, but I'm exhausted enough as is. If I drink any of that, I'll pass out quicker than hell. Besides, we have some things to discuss."

The Chieftain lifted the cups a few inches, looking at each of them individually before turning his gaze back on her. "These? These are mine, but thanks for thinking so highly of me. I appreciate it." Arryn laughed, and he winked at her in response. "So, what's this we need to discuss?"

Arryn recapped what she had just told Cathillian, and the Chieftain didn't seem a bit surprised. He only nodded and *mmhmm*ed in response.

"Alaric has a brother west of here. As far as I knew, they didn't quite get along, but I suppose blood runs thick. Though they're headed out of the Dark Forest, I doubt we'll be lucky enough for them to stay that way. I would have to assume they're going for aid."

"Still, that gives us time to figure out what the hell we need to do with the Arcadians," Cathillian said. "I say we stay alert, but it sounds to me like we've just gotten a free pass."

Arryn smiled. "Yes, it does."

Narrowing his eyes, Cathillian asked, "Why do you seem so excited about this? It's good news, but you seem more excited than cautiously relieved."

Arryn jabbed a finger in his chest. "Because now *we* can go to the Heights."

"The Heights?" the Chieftain asked. "Ah. You hope to speak with the mystics there."

Arryn nodded. "Elysia, Amelia, and I talked about it briefly this morning after sending off the governor and his son, but I didn't really think it would be a possibility for a while—not with the Arcadians to the east and the dark druids to the south. We were pretty much surrounded by the threat of war. How long will it take the dark druids to reach the Terres Forest?

The Chieftain thought for a few moments, taking a long drink from one of his cups. "I would have to say a week and a half or more. That forest is northwest of here. If they could travel through our lands, it would be roughly a week, but they will have to travel all the way west into the Terresian Plains before heading north to avoid our lands entirely."

Lifting her hands and smiling excitedly, Arryn said, "Yes. Perfect! That's more than enough time. We can head south first thing in the morning. It'll take us about three days to get to the southern mountains, and another day to get up to Craigston. I bet Samuel would love to go home for a bit. He hasn't been home since before the Battle for Arcadia began."

Cathillian was quiet as he contemplated the plan. "You're not going anywhere without me—I hope you know that. I'm never letting you go on an adventure by yourself again. You scared the hell out of me!"

Arryn laughed. "First of all, it sucked, but I made it back okay. All in one piece. Secondly, I planned to take you. That's why I said '*we.*' As in you, me, Amelia, Celine, Samuel, and Maddie, too, if she wants to go, but it seems she's enjoying hanging out with the Chieftain and the kids. She's a good teacher. Suits her."

"Where're we goin'?" Samuel asked, holding a cup of wine in each of his hands as well. She realized in that moment he had taken drinking tips from the Chieftain—not that a rearick needed them.

Sighing, Arryn said, "I'm not saying this again. I'm tired. Cathillian, rally the troops. We'll tell everyone at one time."

"Yes, ma'am," Cathillian said, with a slight inflection of sarcasm. "You've been *very* bossy since you've been back, too."

"Shut yer mouth, lad. Ye know ye like it," Samuel said with a drunken wink, several drops of wine dripping down his beard.

"Sweet Queen Bitch," Arryn said with a roll of her eyes. "Just do it."

As Arryn turned her back, she smiled, excitement bubbling in her chest and stomach.

CHAPTER SIX

Two days had passed since the governor and his son had departed the Dark Forest. Though they knew just how dangerous the Forest could be, the ride had been rather peaceful. Now, as they drew closer to Cella, the governor's anxiety kicked up.

The remnant were cold, ruthless beings. They were all that was left of those who had gone mad long ago. Their minds had never fully recovered, and it left them unable to feel anything other than rage and lust for blood, sex, or any other thing they could get their hands on.

Was it possible for them to be understanding about the fact that Talia had been killed? Could they see it as a necessary evil and accept her death as a good thing?

Something told him that would not be the case.

As they closed in on Cella, he became even more grateful that the druid warriors had been forced on him. While he wasn't exactly certain just how effective they would be against a horde of remnant—if the monstrous leader chose to bring that many— he knew he and his son would stand a much better chance *with* them than without.

"What happens if there are a lot of them?" the governor asked.

Cassondra rode a little closer. "Well, if there are a lot of them, we'll play it by ear. I would suggest you not go too close. If they seem hostile, we'll be ready, but we won't engage unless they do. Just do your best not to agitate them. That's easier said than done with the remnant, but it's the best advice we can offer. If the worst should happen, and they attack, retreat will be our only option."

"Retreat? Don't you think they'll chase us?" he asked.

She smiled. "They may be crazed killers, but they aren't going to be anywhere near as fast on foot as our horses can travel. Not only that, but they aren't stupid. They won't approach the Dark Forest."

The outline of the city came into view then, but that wasn't the only thing. He could see a line of men—though he couldn't tell how many—standing by the gate. He had expected them to get there shortly after their own arrival, since it had been exactly a week. They had left the Dark Forest in just enough time to get back.

Still, he expected to be the one waiting, not the other way around. This wasn't the opportunity he had hoped for.

"The remnant are outside the animal control part of our nature abilities, as well as outside the mental abilities of the mystics. They're neither beast nor human. That being said, I can sense them. Their darkness. I would say there are twenty or so," Cassondra said.

The governor took a deep breath, letting it out in a shaky sigh. "I don't have a very good feeling about this."

"Everything will be fine, Father," Nathaniel said. The governor looked at his son, who had a confident look on his face. "We have the best warriors in the Valley with us. Everything will be fine."

Unable to speak, and knowing he didn't share his son's confidence, the governor only managed a smile and curt nod before facing forward again.

As they approached, the remnant he had spoken with before stepped forward out of the group of beasts surrounding him. Holding up his hand, the governor signaled for everyone he traveled with to stay behind as he rode his horse a few paces farther before dismounting.

The governor nodded. "Good evening," he said, though he knew the greeting would be wasted on them.

"Well? Where is she?" the remnant asked, his words short and to the point.

The governor swallowed as he looked at the monster's red eyes and hideous skin. It was covered in boils, sweat, and oil, as well as patches of dirt, filth, and what he could only imagine was blood. He only hoped the creature had killed a deer on the way, instead of the alternative.

"Okay," the governor began, "so, several things have happened since I last saw you. I rode to Arcadia in hopes of finding the truth, and I found it. Everything you said was true. Talia had taken over the city, and Scarlett had helped her. Unfortunately, shortly after my arrival a young woman Talia had tried to kill came back seeking revenge."

The governor paused, allowing those words to sink in. It would have been obvious to anyone else what he was saying, and he hoped it would be to the remnant as well. Unfortunately, that wasn't quite the case.

The remnant's blood-red eyes narrowed as he stared the governor down. "And?"

The governor took a deep breath and did his best to continue to look confident, though he knew he had blown any chance of that happening before he had even stepped down from the horse.

"The girl. She killed Talia. If it's any consolation, she took her head. She killed several of Talia's followers, too. One of them was even ripped apart by her tiger."

There was a pause as the remnant took a step forward.

"Easy, *beast*," Cassondra spat the harsh words from close

behind the governor. The druids had left their horses and came closer. "We mean no harm, but if we sense any dark intent we *will* take action."

The remnant leaned to the side, his eyes finding the dominant female several feet behind the governor. "I see you brought friends. Didn't trust me?" he asked, a dark smile on his face.

Standing downwind as he was, the governor got a whiff of his breath. It smelled of death and decay, since his teeth were rotted in several places and broken away in others. His gums were the color of blood, and were seeping what looked like a bloodied pus-like liquid down what was left of his teeth as his lips put pressure on them.

Stifling a gag, the governor said, "It seems you didn't trust me either."

"Get the bitch. That was all ya had to do." The remnant licked his cracked lips. "I traveled a long way for nothin'. Me and my brothers are hungry."

Doing his best not to show his fear, the governor said, "The ones behind me aren't just *any* people. They're druids of the Dark Forest. I wouldn't do anything, if I were you. I came here because we had a deal. Because when I make a deal, I keep it. That's the kind of man I am. I *never* promised you I would bring Talia back. In fact, I told you I didn't know if I could. What I *did* promise was information. And I delivered. Talia is dead. Scarlett runs the city. I can't promise Scarlett either, but I might be able to get the others to separate the mystic from the fight and deliver her to you. *Might*."

The remnant let out a deep belly laugh, his head falling back and his breath nearly choking the governor again. Almost as if a switch had been flipped, his head snapped back in position, all humor gone from his expression. "That was your last chance. You didn't deliver."

By the time the governor heard the sound of the axe cutting

through the air, it was too late. One of the remnant behind the leader had thrown it upon hearing his leader's words.

The governor's head whirled around just in time to see the axe cleave deeply into the chest of his horse, the animal crying out before falling to the ground, struggling and in pain.

From that moment on, everything moved so quickly he could scarcely make sense of it. Something wrapped around his entire body and yanked him backward. He looked down just in time to see vines unraveling after having placed him on the back of another horse.

He looked back up to see the leader of the remnant caught in vines before being thrown back several feet. Ryel and Cassondra dropped to the ground, laying hands on the horse as Clara began growing the grass long enough to tangle the feet of any remnant who were close enough.

The druids on the ground had been fast, not only healing the horse, but giving it back the energy that had been wasted in its struggle to fight the pain. The horse jumped to its feet, fleeing toward the Dark Forest.

He watched as another horse ran forward, Ryel and Cassondra mounting before thrusting their hands forward. Thick vines continued to burst from the ground, grabbing remnant limbs and pulling them to the ground.

Several remnant lost an arm, a leg, or both. All the governor could do was sit there in awe, his eyes wide and his jaw hanging open.

The druids never ceased to amaze him, their skill ever reminding him just how deadly they really were.

"Dad!"

The governor's son grabbed his arm. Nathaniel's horse was facing in the opposite direction of his own—the direction they needed to flee in. He blinked hard, bringing himself back to the present.

"We have to go. *Now!*" Nathaniel said.

CANDY CRUM & MICHAEL ANDERLE

"*Go!*" Cassondra shouted from in front of them.

Without warning, the horse responded to the druid's order and spun, taking off in the direction they had come from. The governor rode silently beside his son for nearly a mile before they saw the horse that had been injured waiting ahead of them.

Without instructions, their horses slowed as well.

"What's going on?" Nathaniel asked. "Shouldn't we continue?"

The governor shook his head. "They must have told the horses to go only this far and wait. I don't know, son. I don't understand how any of their magic works."

Nathaniel snorted. "Yeah, well, I'm starting to think they had it right all along. I've never seen anything like that before."

Only a few minutes later, the sound of hoofbeats echoed around them, and they saw the last horse, which was carrying both Ryel and Cassondra. Without any verbal communication, their horse stopped, Cassondra getting off and making her way to the beautiful animal the governor had ridden earlier.

"Is she gonna be okay?" the governor asked.

Cassondra smiled. "Are you kidding? She's got more energy right now than any of us. We left some pretty pissed-off remnant back there. We need to get out of here. *Fast.*"

The governor sighed in relief. "You don't have to tell me twice. Did I mention how grateful I am that you strong-armed me into letting you come?"

She winked and smiled. "Maybe you can repay me after all this with a free trip to the city and a hot shower. Cathillian hasn't shut up about them since he's been back."

Without a word having been spoken, all the horses broke into a gallop. The governor, riding just behind her, smiled. After several paces he said, "I think that can be arranged. Well, provided I have a city to go back to after all this is said and done."

CHAPTER SEVEN

Though her excitement had gotten the upper hand, Arryn felt apprehension, too, as she said her goodbyes. Once again, she was forced to watch Elysia tear up as the Elder said goodbye to her son and the young woman she had raised.

Arryn could only smile and tell Elysia this trip would be different. It was only a short fact-finding trip. They certainly didn't plan to be gone long, and waiting would have been a terrible mistake. With the dark druids gone, they were temporarily safer than they had been in a very long time.

A heavy sigh had escaped Elysia then, her eyes rolling as a tear fell down each cheek. "Fine. Whatever you say. I still don't like it, and I still wish I could go with you."

Arryn had just barely held back any evidence of her own worries about what traveling would bring, but she managed, knowing her strength and confidence were the only things holding Elysia together.

It had been two days since they had left the safety of the Dark Forest, and they were making much better time than expected. The weather had been warm enough at night, and in the early mornings that shivering hadn't sapped the energy they had gained from sleep. The horses regained energy after only short stops and a quick burst of magic to pep them up.

With the druids refreshed by a few hours' rest, their magic fully accessible and recharged, giving the equivalent of a magical jolt of kaffe to the horses was a breeze.

Arryn silently urged Snow forward, matching their pace to Samuel's. "So, how long do you think we have?"

The rearick smiled. "Ah, lass, I'd say we'll make it before nightfall. At least ta the mountains. The trip up'll take some real effort fer the horses, but they'll do all right."

She nodded, a bit relieved to hear it. While she enjoyed going on trips, she didn't much care for the unknown. She had never been south, so Craigston and the Heights were a mystery to her.

Like the druids of the Dark Forest, Arcadians had been taught to be wary of the mystics. After what she had learned about them, she couldn't say she blamed anyone for being afraid of them.

She wondered if the city would turn on mystics altogether once they freed Arcadia from Scarlett. It wouldn't be entirely unreasonable, especially if the Arcadians learned what had actually been done to them, but she hoped they wouldn't shun an entire group of people based on the evil of a few.

That was a worry for another day.

As they traveled, the road that led from Craigston to Arcadia came into view. Arryn sighed in relief, knowing they were getting closer. She was about to mention as much to Samuel when he tightened his hands on the reins and kicked at the sides of his horse.

Arryn glanced behind her to find looks of confusion that mirrored her own, then turned back and gave Snow a mental shove. The tiger leapt forward, her long, powerful legs propelling them after Samuel at speeds even the horses couldn't match.

Within only a few seconds, Arryn caught up to him, but she didn't need to ask why he had taken off. She could see the reason.

Ahead on the road were rearick fighting what looked like

Arcadians. Given the way they were dressed, though, she assumed they were more likely from the small villages that were scattered throughout the Valley, or even from farmhouses.

Dozens of rearick fought twice that number of Valley men amid carts that were probably filled with the amphorald crystals the Chancellor had ordered as soon as the factory was up and running.

It was a good sign that the city was still functioning, even under the new management, but that was about it. The crystals were supposed to be used to create magitech lighting for the homes they were building in the Boulevard, but these would more than likely go to magitech weapons.

"You take the right, and I'll go left. The others will catch up," Arryn shouted.

Samuel only nodded in response as he steered his horse to the right of the battle. Arryn focused, a silent signal from Snow to hold on tight making her get a better hold on the tiger's fur.

Once she was near the battle, Snow let out a monstrous growl and leapt into the air to pounce on the first person Arryn had targeted. The bond was fun and amusing in private, giving her a comfortable feeling that she was never truly alone.

But in the face of danger, it became something else.

The tiger became an extension of herself, something she had been told about, but had never expected to experience herself. It was almost like being in two places at once. The connection allowing Arryn to fight twice as many—or more—enemies at once, since she was able to target them for the tiger without a word being spoken.

Excitement and pride welled in Arryn's chest as she and her colossal, magical beast went airborne, eager to test their bond in their first true battle together. What they had accomplished in Arcadia the night Arryn had killed Talia had been stealthy, but not what she would consider true battle.

This would be.

A tall man looked up, his eyes widening and his cocked fist dropping as he realized what was about to happen to him. Snow's paws—each twice the size of his face—hit his chest as she descended, taking him to the ground as her powerful jaws bit down on his head.

Blood sprayed into the air as Arryn jumped from Snow's back and landed on her hands. She collapsed her arms to somersault once and rolled onto her knees, bow in hand before the tiger and her target had even hit the ground.

Arryn released her first arrow, aiming high because the rearick were short. It pierced through the back of the man's skull and dropped him. She was no mystic and therefore couldn't read thoughts, but nature magic allowed her to sense the good and bad in others.

These men were dark. They weren't much better than the remnant she had encountered. They were only better-looking, though that wasn't saying much with this group.

Arryn released three more arrows before anyone realized a woman was taking them down one by one.

A growl sounded out, causing Arryn to spin and grab for the ram's horn-handled knife in her belt, but it wasn't needed. Blood spattered Arryn's face, coating whatever hadn't been hit by Snow's last kill.

A body hit the ground in front of Arryn with a heavy *thump* as she blew air hard out of her mouth, trying to use the blast to rid her lips of some of the arterial spray before wiping the rest away.

Reaching up, Arryn cleaned her pursed lips and squinted eyes before looking into the icy blue orbs of her familiar, who seemed surprisingly apologetic.

"You know, I'd like to *not* wear at least one of your victims. If you could manage that, I'd sure appreciate it," Arryn said, a sarcastic tone to her voice.

The tiger's mouth opened only a little, a low rumble coming out that Arryn translated into, "Then save *yourself* next time."

Arryn's eyes widened as she saw several men pile onto Samuel, war hammers, axes, and swords raised.

"*Snow!*" Arryn shouted, pointing.

The tiger didn't wait for another word, turning and leaping toward the group.

"Bitch!"

Arryn finished pulling the knife from the back of her belt, dropped her bow, and turned on her knees in time to narrowly avoid a hammer smashing down next to her. She thrust forward, the knife easily sinking into the man's belly.

"Thanks for the compliment. She's quite the badass. Tell her I said hello before she sends you to hell," Arryn responded, pulling the knife free and shoving it through the spongy part of his chin straight into his brain.

She yanked it out, allowing his body to drop to the ground as a fireball whizzed past her head. She saw Amelia to her left, eyes as black as night and a fireball in one hand. Another orb was quickly replacing the one she had thrown with only the flick of her wrist.

You look terrifying—like you bathe in the blood of your enemies, Amelia sent to Arryn.

With a smile, Arryn nodded in Amelia's direction. *Good. That's what I want them to think,* she sent back. She wiped the blood from her blade before sheathing it and pulled her staff from her back.

"Come and get it, boys!" she shouted, garnering the attention of several men in her general area.

Cathillian urged Maia, his horse, to run as fast as she could. He had seen Arryn and Snow take off after Samuel, but he hadn't understood what was happening. There couldn't have been anything wrong, or Arryn would have said something.

Within moments, the sounds of battle—faint as they were from that distance—reached his ears, and he understood.

Samuel must have seen the battle.

Upon realizing that, he urged Maia ahead of the others and saw what the rearick had—countless men fighting on the road.

Worry seizing him, Cathillian repeated Arryn's actions, taking off in a flash and leaving everyone else behind—or so he thought.

Amelia stayed right beside him; more than likely she had listened to his thoughts as he figured out what was taking place. While he didn't like the idea of someone in his head, he was grateful for it then.

Amelia's horse was faster, and she was on the ground before Cathillian arrived. He clearly hadn't taken care of Maia quite as well as he had thought, and made a mental note to remedy that later.

Amelia threw her first fireball as Cathillian stopped to find Arryn. Fear gripped him when he saw the violence, but didn't see her. Blood, insides, and dead bodies littered the ground, but Arryn was nowhere to be seen.

She's fine, Amelia sent to him, quickly followed by the image of Arryn standing in the middle of four men. Her staff whirled, parrying their attacks as she landed blow after blow. She looked like a dancer as she moved. *She doesn't need you, Cat. Stop worrying.*

He wanted to argue, but he knew Amelia was right. He also knew that his worry for her could cost someone else their life. He needed to help that someone else.

Turning for the opposite side of the battle Amelia had shown him, knowing Arryn and Amelia had that side covered, he began to run, pulling his sword free of its sheath on his side.

Though he hadn't seen Snow, he heard a loud growl rip through the air just before a rearick fell from the sky and landed at Cathillian's feet. He stopped in his tracks.

It was Samuel.

"Holy shit, man!" Cathillian said, his eyes widening as he dropped to the ground to help his friend. "What the hell?"

Samuel grumbled as he rolled to his belly, then got up on his hands and knees. He was covered in cuts, bruises, and a lot of blood, but otherwise he seemed fine.

"That damned cat of Arryn's," Samuel grumbled.

Cathillian's brows creased. "What?"

Samuel looked at him incredulously. "That furry she-beast apparently didn't think I could handle me own fight. She showed up outta nowhere 'n started cuttin' men down before grabbin' onta me backside and throwin' me outta the way."

Cathillian clapped a hand over his mouth, trying desperately not to laugh at the rearick. The tiger had continued to grow even after reaching the Dark Forest, though the cub remained the same size, despite his mutual bond with Arryn.

He hadn't even grown naturally, remaining stunted in size—though no one seemed to mind. He was quite adorable and had won the hearts of everyone in the villages.

Though it seemed that Snow had finally stopped growing, she was big enough now Arryn could ride her even more easily. The cat could almost look Chaos, Elysia's horse and oversized familiar, in the eye.

He imagined the tiger—big as she was—locking her jaws around Samuel's waist and literally throwing him out of the way.

Finally, he lost his battle and began laughing, his head falling back as he howled at the mental images.

"Ah, fuck ye!" Samuel said. He threw a hand out and hit Cathillian in the shoulder, effectively knocking the laughing druid off-balance. "Her mouth is a *lot* bigger 'n it looks. Crazy beast. I'll show her."

A shadow fell over them, and Cathillian's laughter immediately halted. A low rumble echoed as both men looked up to see the tiger, covered in blood and filth, glaring at the rearick.

Cathillian swallowed, realizing just how terrifying she looked. "Uh... she says you're an ungrateful little beast."

Samuel's eyes widened at Cathillian before he turned toward the tiger, jumping to his feet and pointing a finger at her. Even at full height, the rearick was still a few inches too short to look her directly in the eye, which only made his anger and threat more amusing. Once again, Cathillian was on the verge of tears from laughter.

"Listen here, lassie," Samuel started, but he was quickly interrupted.

There was a loud, angry shout from the edge of the battle and Snow let out an ear-piercing, pain-filled cry of her own. As soon as she did, Cathillian snapped to attention. He heard Arryn's pained cry over the sounds of battle as well.

Without a doubt, she had felt Snow's injury.

Cathillian leapt up as Snow's head whirled, throwing the bloodied battle axe she had just pulled from her shoulder to the side. She took a step forward, lowered her head, and roared so loudly that Cathillian could actually feel the vibrations in the air around him.

The man who had thrown it suddenly looked terrified, his eyes widening as he turned to run. Unfortunately for him, his axe hadn't left more than a scratch on an animal like Snow.

She pounced, easily covering the fifty or more feet between her and her target. She landed on him with all her weight and crushed him instantly, though she still bit down on him, ending his life as she pulled him apart.

Cathillian almost threw up when she dropped the top half of his body, his guts spilling onto the ground beneath him.

"I need to get to Arryn," Cathillian said, trying to distract himself. "I know she can fight, but she felt Snow get hurt. She's distracted."

Samuel nodded. "Aye. Keep our girl safe."

Without another word, both men headed back into battle. As

he ran forward, Cathillian saw a young rearick boy hiding next to a cart with his knees tucked into his chest and tears streaming down his face. He couldn't have been more than five or six.

A heavy sigh of horror left his throat, and his heart broke for the young boy. Looking around, Cathillian immediately judged the scene before him and formulated a plan to get the boy out.

"Thank the Bitch you're here." Cathillian turned to see Celine. "I've been trying to find a way to get him out of there, but I'm not that great in hand-to-hand yet. If I threw a fireball they'd be on me like a remnant on a fat man."

"How good are you with magic?" Cathillian asked.

Celine smiled darkly, her eyes flashing black after a single blink. "Trust me, nephew, you won't have anything to worry about. Get the boy; I'll handle the rest."

He smiled because she called him 'nephew,' though he knew that little expression would have earned him a punch from Arryn.

He and Celine had been in battle together only once, on the way back to the Dark Forest when they had fled Arcadia. He hadn't seen her fight, though she had certainly done a good enough job—that was evident enough from her not dying.

After having spent time with Elysia, Nika, and eventually Arryn once she had returned, Celine was learning more and more all the time.

Without any hesitation at all, Cathillian trusted her.

He nodded once before running straight into the fray. He didn't pay a single bit of attention to the men running after him, knowing Celine would be watching.

As men ran for him, Cathillian looked straight at the boy. In his peripheral vision, he saw shards of razor-sharp ice ripping through the attackers as they approached. He silently took a moment to be impressed by her control—she had missed him entirely—as he dropped to his knees and slid to a stop in front of the boy.

CANDY CRUM & MICHAEL ANDERLE

"It's okay. I'm here to help you," Cathillian said.

The boy was terribly afraid and looked at Cathillian like he might lash out at him at any moment, but slowly, he extended his hand toward the druid.

Bodies dropped around him, and he turned to see both Celine and Amelia, their black eyes focused, throwing fireballs and blades of ice to protect him.

Cathillian grabbed the boy and ran for the women behind him. At that moment, he realized it was the women holding down the battle and not the men.

Arryn had run in without hesitation and started dropping men right and left, and her familiar had thrown their one male ally to safety. All Cathillian had done was rescue a kid; the women had protected him from behind the lines.

He found it kind of badass.

It was strange for him to be so useless, but instead of feeling that way he actually felt pride. He would head into battle with them any day.

As soon as he set the boy down behind Celine and Amelia, Cathillian said, "Now, if it's all good, I'd like to get my hands dirty. I've been rather useless, except for saving an innocent little boy."

Amelia smiled. "Go right ahead. Or, you could continue to play search and rescue and use that magic of yours to get fallen rearick to safety."

He sighed and smiled. "Yes, ma'am."

SNOW POUNCED ON ARRYN, knocking her to the ground before catching a sword in her mouth. Arryn saw blood drip from her already gory mouth as she lunged for the man.

Arryn had suffered several bruises as well as a broken arm and nose that she had healed under Snow's protection, but she was undamaged otherwise. Feeling exhausted, she jumped to her feet and looked around.

Cathillian was checking the fallen for signs of life. When he found them, vines burst from the ground outside the skirmish and swooped in to grab the injured rearick before pulling him free of the battlefield.

There weren't many enemies left, but there were several dead or injured rearick on the ground. They wouldn't have the ability to heal them all, and it crushed her to realize that.

Arryn raised her staff and swung it, cracking a large man on the side of the head. He fell, and she raised her staff over her head before bringing it down hard on his once again.

Screams and cheers erupted, and she turned to see those left standing—covered in blood, filth, and only the goddess herself knew what else—smiling, their fists and weapons raised over their heads.

With a heavy sigh of relief, Arryn collapsed to her knees, allowing exhaustion to take her.

Although barely able to move now that the adrenaline was gone, she lifted her staff into the air and cheered, "Yeah! We didn't fucking die!" before collapsing to her side, smiling as a worried tiger licked the side of her face.

CHAPTER EIGHT

It took more than an hour for Cathillian, Arryn, and Samuel to help heal those on the verge of death just enough that they could withstand the trip back to Craigston.

Luckily for Arryn, she had mainly used physical force instead of relying on her magic. It allowed her to do a bit more than Cathillian and especially Samuel, who had only barely begun to learn to use his gift.

"I didn't want 'nybody ta know I'd been practicin'," Samuel said, "but when I saw me brothers damn near dead, I figured nunna that mattered."

Arryn felt as though he was holding something back, but she let it go, knowing the rearick had overcome a large hurdle by admitting he had an affinity for magic at all.

Healing was hard to learn. Even the druids didn't learn how to do it right out the gate. Growing and creating plants was how things usually got started. Healing came much later.

Samuel was an anomaly. He had begun with one of the more difficult things to learn, though he hadn't tried anything else as far as she knew.

Arryn was exhausted, both physically *and* mentally, now that she had used so much magic. Snow had been wounded several times, and she had been Arryn's first priority.

Once the battle had been concluded, Arryn had healed Snow and sent her off to retrieve Dante from where they had left him when they headed to battle.

Now, everyone rode in silence, having reached the vast southern hills that led up the mountains to Craigston and the Heights.

They were certainly moving a bit slower now, but it seemed that they would make it to the rearick town shortly after nightfall. Samuel had said that there was a lake close to his home where she and Snow could bathe and clean the blood off. They had been covered worse than anyone.

Dante yawned from the ground below his mother as they walked, and Arryn almost laughed at him. He was a cute little guy, and his size puzzled her, but he made her happy. He was still very young and dependent on his mother, and he tired quickly on long walks.

Snow stopped and Arryn pulled Dante onto his mother's massive back right along with her.

"Samuel," Arryn said, her voice forced because of how tired she was.

"Yeah?" he replied, putting just as much effort into speaking.

"I hope you're ready for this," she replied, a dreamy smile on her face as her eyes looked upward to the stars beginning to glow in the night sky.

"Ready fer what, lass?"

"I'm gonna snore *so* loud. It's gonna be bad. Snow says I snore like an old man when I'm this tired," Arryn told him.

The rearick would have laughed, had he not been on the verge of passing out. "We'll have a contest then. Whoever gets punched first is the winner. And how did she know what an old man's snoring sounds like?"

"How is getting punched first a good... *Oh*. Because they're the loudest. Got it. Damn it all, I'm tired. I can't even put simple thoughts together." Arryn yawned. "Snow heard the Chieftain sawing logs on her way back from a hunt. When I laughed at the images she relayed, she basically told me I shouldn't laugh because I'm just as bad."

Samuel did laugh then. "Yep. A contest it'll be, lass, because I'm about ta shake the damn windas once we get ta Craigston."

SCARLETT SMILED as the sheets were pulled back and her companion moved up to lie next to her. "That was perfect," was all she said, catching her breath.

Barbara smiled, her blonde hair spreading over her pillow as she pulled the sheets over them. "I was happy to be of service. You seemed tense."

With a chuckle, Scarlett said, "Yes, well, once everything is all settled and Amelia and that druid girl are dead, my stress will melt away. It will all be nothing more than a bad memory. We're climbing the hill now, but don't worry. We're almost to the top."

"Not that I doubt you, but how do you figure?"

The wicked mystic shrugged her naked shoulders. "See, everything we're doing now, everything we have been working on... All the brainwashing, the compulsion, the subtle and not-so-subtle suggestions... The Boulevard is being rebuilt now, and as I continue to put my efforts into positive things in the city, the people will grow to love me. The mystical magic is the glue that their emotions and loyalty to me stick to. Talia had the right idea, just not the power to pull it off."

Barbara nodded, her green eyes glistening in the candlelight. "But the Chancellor and the nature bitch both have to die for that to happen."

Scarlett nodded. "Amelia and Arryn could expose me. It wouldn't take much, because our hold on the people is light. Too many of them, and too few of us. Those two could point out how closely I worked with Talia. They could point out a great many things, and brick by brick my entire façade would tumble until the wall was nothing but rubble below my feet.

"But once they're gone—once no one is left to stand in my way—we can drop the magic. It won't be needed any longer. I can live here and rule over the people with absolutely no resistance. They will love me. They will do anything I ask them to, and they will believe their fearless Amelia died a traitor to the city right along with Arryn."

Barbara smiled, turning to lie on her side. Her hand came to rest on Scarlett's bare arm, her fingertips gently grazing the sensitive skin along the crease of her elbow.

"Simply tell me anything you need, and I'll do it. You know this," Barbara said.

There was a knock at the door before Nikolai walked in, not waiting for an answer. Neither woman bothered to cover herself further, since neither was very modest.

"Yes, Nikolai?" Scarlett asked.

Nikolai smiled. "You asked for an update as soon as I had one. Well, I do."

Scarlett sat up, the sheet falling to her waist. "What is it?"

"The Guard. We have worked on them night after night, and I think they are bending. Whatever they'd heard about Arryn and the time she spent training the men to fight is all gone. Nothing is left except anger and hatred. Though, we might have had to do some convincing."

Scarlett hadn't needed to use much mental energy since the arrival of her friends, so it was easy for her to push against the barrier Nikolai had raised. He had nothing to hide, but they kept their minds hidden enough from one another that general absentminded thoughts weren't often heard.

Feeling the brush, Nikolai lowered his barrier and allowed Scarlett to see what they had done.

As he had said for several nights now, they had snuck into the barracks after dark and planted subtle thoughts in the minds of the guardsmen. When they were sleeping, it took little to no effort to push their influence, though it took repetition.

They had moved from barracks to barracks, exerting only minor compulsion. It had taken the entire night, every night, and it had been painfully exhausting, but after almost a week they had decided to seal their work.

Nikolai, Vanessa, and Theo had all disguised themselves as their enemies, having picked their identities from the minds of those closest to them. Vanessa played the part of Arryn, Nikolai was Amelia, and Theo had been Cathillian.

They broke into the barracks as quietly as always. Nikolai made his way to a bed, mentally shoving the man lying in it to wake him. As the man awoke, Nikolai made sure his hand was tight around the Guard's throat, convincing him that he was being choked by their once-faithful leader, Amelia.

Once the man had passed out with the image of the angry and cold-blooded Amelia burned into his mind, Nikolai let go, leaving him alive and unharmed. He hadn't wanted to kill the man, only make him think he was dying—and that Amelia had been the murderer.

Across the walkway, Theo and Vanessa attacked a Guard they knew had been close to Cathillian. Just as Nikolai had done, the two mystics allowed the man to get a good look at their faces but left him alive.

Theo cracked him in the head with the butt of a magitech rifle that had been in the corner, physically knocking him out instead of using magic.

Last but not least, magically keeping all the other men sound asleep, they went through and slit the throats of several of the guards. As those men were bleeding out in their beds, the mystics implanted memories in the remaining ten guards' minds.

They convinced them that they had woken to the sound of

their brothers being killed, causing Amelia, Arryn, and Cathillian to flee.

The three mystics left the barracks, standing outside before giving every living man in there the mental shove to wake up, terrified and alert to what happened.

As Scarlett pulled back from Nikolai's mind, she reached to her left and touched a small magitech lamp next to her, triggering the amphorald crystal inside to light. She saw that Nikolai was covered in blood.

She smiled.

"You know, I thought of that very scenario not just a day or two ago. Were you peeking?"

Nikolai returned her smile and lowered his head in a slow nod, his eyes momentarily closing before he met her gaze again. "I did. I apologize, but you seemed so deep in thought, so worried about how you might pull it off."

"I *was* worried about all of you. I certainly couldn't have done that myself, and knowing the three of you were on barracks duty while Barbara and I kept Henry in line and managed the citizens… Well, I just couldn't bear to ask any more of you than I already had. I had assumed it would be too much. I wouldn't risk it."

He smiled. "That was why I did this for you. A little patience —that was all we needed. We spent several days preparing. We only needed sufficient meditation, drink, and rest, which we got plenty of late last night and earlier today. We pulled it off brilliantly. Right now, those men are scouting the city. I'm sure you're about to have even more visitors."

Scarlett couldn't believe it. Nikolai had plucked the plan straight from her head and had executed it perfectly. Those men were now convinced, without a shred of doubt, that that it had been Amelia, Arryn, and Cathillian that had broken into the city, killed all those guards and attempted to kill two others.

The two who were alive would give positive identification,

while the others would swear to seeing them flee the barracks and the city. It was all too perfect. The Guard would now listen to her.

Before anything else could be said, frantic pounding on the front door to her home echoed through the halls and into her room. The three mystics took turns looking at one another, smiles growing on their faces.

"Nikolai, dear, you're covered in blood. Please use my shower. Barbara, it's your turn now. Disguise yourself as a guard—my personal guard. Greet the men, and tell them I'm getting dressed."

Barbara leaned over, kissing Scarlett on the shoulder before getting up. Without dressing, the mystic stood and walked across the room.

Scarlett couldn't see the white take her lover's eyes, but she could sense her power as the woman's body began to change. She walked into the darkness of the hallway, heading to greet the eager guests.

CHAPTER NINE

B y the time Samuel led the others into the rearick town of Craigston, every one of them were ready to pass out. Exhaustion had completely taken some, like Arryn, who had fallen asleep on the back of her fearless tiger, Snow. Dante was out, too.

Cathillian had been only barely able to hang on, but Samuel was even worse. He hadn't grown in strength like the others. His magic was still new, so any use at all zapped him entirely. But that didn't matter—he'd had to stay awake to lead everyone to safety and get help for the injured.

Unfortunately, several rearick lost their lives that day, but Samuel was grateful they had been able to save the ones they had. It had been an honor to help his own people for once.

He didn't mind working with the Arcadians or the druids. To him, assisting the Arcadians helped his own people by proxy. What was good for those selfish bastards in the city would bring profitable work to his brothers.

The druids, however, were different. They weren't selfish. They weren't bad folk at all. They were everything the rearick were—although a bit taller and prettier, of course—honorable, kind, and possessed of sharp tongues and wit. All things that made a man or woman trustworthy.

He supposed they were a bit more organized in the battle department, too, though he would never tell the young pointy-eared lad that. He knew Cathillian would never let him hear the end of it.

Samuel loved Arryn. She was kind of like a daughter to him, though he would have been a very young father to her. He felt the pride and closeness to her that he had felt for his own child.

She was everything he hoped his daughter, Alyssa, would have been when she grew up—minus the magic, of course. It was kind of appropriate, given how he felt about Arryn's aunt—yet another thing he would never admit to.

But his love for Arryn and his confusing feelings for Celine—that he still refused to admit, even to himself—were very different from what he felt for Cathillian. While Arryn was like his daughter, Cathillian was like a brother.

They constantly went back and forth with one another, arguing and picking on one another. If Cathillian had ever failed to give Samuel a hard time, he would surely have taken offense. Tall as a tree or not, that boy was like a rearick. Stubborn, feisty, and strong—not to mention funny as hell.

Samuel had lost his family quite some time ago, but he had stumbled into another one.

"Ugh."

Samuel heard the moans and groans of discontent behind him. He looked back and saw Arryn waking as she nearly fell from Snow. The big cat had turned her head and was trying to nudge Arryn back up, but it wasn't happening.

"Yer about ta take a spill, lassie," Samuel said.

She groaned again. "Please tell me we're almost there."

The rearick laughed. "We just made it. Ophelia's is just ahead, if anyone wants ta make a stop."

Arryn perked up then, raising one hand as the other rubbed

her eyes. "Me." She coughed, clearing her throat. He laughed at her again because she looked so pathetic. "Me. I wanna go. I want some mystic's brew."

Samuel's eyes widened as the corners of his mouth turned up. "*Ye* wanna drink? Ye *never* drink."

She laughed. "Yeah, well, I sure as hell will now. I love the Chieftain, but that shit he makes would strip the bark off a tree. He makes two kinds—sweet enough with the sugar cane to blacken your teeth on contact, or bitter enough to eat a hole through your stomach."

"It ain't the shit we make here or the shit those mystics up the hill make, I'll give ye that," Samuel said, "but I rather liked it. I was impressed."

Arryn looked at him incredulously, her hands making a sarcastic gesture.

Samuel laughed. "Right. I see yer point."

"Exactly. The way I heard it, rearick could eat the ass out of a skunk and those cast-iron bellies wouldn't even grumble about it," Arryn said.

Samuel opened his mouth to protest, but he shut it again. "Ye know, I don't have an argument fer that, lass. It's true."

Arryn smiled. "See? So, I want something good before I pass out."

With a nod, Samuel said, "Come on. I'll get ye good and drunk. Ye won't even know yer own name when we're done."

"Uh..." Cathillian chimed in. "Do you think that's a good idea? You're exhausted."

"Butt out, lad," Samuel said. "The lady wants to let go and have some fun. She ain't had a bit of it since she got back from that damnable mountain. I think she's earned it."

Arryn found a little energy then, smiling with excitement as they grew closer to the building Samuel had pointed out.

"I didn't even think about it, but this really *is* the first time I've let myself relax," Arryn said.

"Maybe we should find ye somethin' to punch while we're in there," Samuel said.

"*Samuel!*" Cathillian scolded.

"Damn it, boy," Samuel snapped, looking back from his horse. He pointed a finger at Cathillian. "In the damned woods we do things yer way. This up here is rearick country. Ye made me respect the trees, fer goddess' sake. Not a single huntin' trip! Ye owe me."

Cathillian laughed. "Damn, Sam. Get all feisty about it, why don't ya?"

Samuel nodded and turned back around with a smile on his face. "I will. So will she, if she likes. Lass, ye don't walk into Ophelia's without plannin' ta punch or break at least *some*thin'."

Arryn almost beamed with excitement. "Hell, yes. Let's get these people to safety and make sure they're taken care of. Then it's time to have some fun."

SPRING HAD COME, and though it was still too cold for most people to swim, it wasn't for Elysia. She liked the water cold, especially in the Kalt River.

Sometimes, when she had thoughts constantly flowing through her mind and raging like that very river, she would slip away after dark for a swim. On this particular night, she'd had quite a bit of the Chieftain's wine, so she was well equipped to handle the cold water.

Elysia stripped off her clothes and stepped forward, dipping her toes into the water. Smiling as she balanced on one foot, she found the water truly was warm enough for the swimming season to begin.

The Elder took slow steps, wading into the water. The current pressed against her, but it wasn't anything she couldn't handle. It was relaxing, the rippling water massaging her body from head to toe.

As she stood there in the moonlight, she thought back to the first time she had ever gone night-swimming. It had been with Cathillian's father, Liam. She smiled as she recalled it.

Druids didn't allow things like chastity to burden them or weigh them down like the Arcadians did. It wasn't as if they spent all their time getting it on in the Forest, but it was a celebration of life—something beautiful between two people. Certainly nothing to be ashamed of.

So, when Liam had snuck into her home to wake her when she was sixteen, stealing her away in the night. It had come as no surprise to the Chieftain when he found her bed empty the next morning.

They had spirited away to the river, laughing as they chased one another. She'd had feelings for Liam since she was a little girl. He was only two years older, but when he had told her how he felt about her, she couldn't stay away.

He was incredibly tall, even for the tall druids, and had long, dark-blonde hair, tanned skin, and emerald eyes. The intense color of his irises was rare, even among the druids, who were all born with green eyes because of their magic.

His magic was strong, but his mental and physical strength in battle were unmatched. It was he who had convinced her to train, though her father had tried fruitlessly for years.

Day in and day out she trained with him. Her skills quickly progressed, but her body was always very sore. Every night, Liam would sneak her away and bring her to the river.

He would walk her in and care for her, healing her as he washed her long hair in the current. Never once did he try to take advantage of the situation, which only made her love him more.

Finally, after months of the routine—training hard during the day and sneaking away to the river at night to be alone—she made the move she had wanted to for so long and became a woman.

It didn't take long for her father to find out, of course, but he handled it well. He liked Liam and what he brought out in Elysia, a fire he had feared had been extinguished when her mother died.

It was on the bank of that very river, only a year later, that she had told Liam that he would be a father. Tears streaked her face as she remembered that day.

Elysia looked over her shoulder at the thick patch of grass just outside the edge of the woods. Liam had planted a large patch of lilies there for her. They had bloomed purple and white—her favorites.

He had grown them for her and their unborn son. Even now, over twenty years later, whatever grew in that area was healthier than anything else in the Forest.

Elysia's eyes widened when they saw not a tall patch of grass, but blooming lilies. The tips of her fingers gently came to rest on her lips. They were bright pink, but they were beautiful.

"Liam," she said into the darkness, "I feel so lost without them here. I wish you could have met Arryn. She's just like our little girl would have been."

She took an unsteady, deep breath, the air catching in her chest and throat several times as she fought more tears.

"They're off on their own, and I'm stuck here. I'm doing nothing. Wading in our spot. What good is that going to do?"

She exhaled hard as she stared at the flowers. The wind blew, chilling her skin where the cold water had touched it.

As she stood there, she closed her eyes, once again focusing on the water massaging her tense body. Her stress began to melt away and her thoughts slowed down, becoming clearer to her.

Elysia was intoxicated. Everything swirled around her, but her current state mixed with the calmness she felt gave her an idea—one she wished she'd had earlier.

Her eyes snapped open as a smile spread across her lips. "I can find out what kind of situation they're going into."

As if lightning had struck her brain, Elysia's eyes flashed green for a moment. The water immediately swirled around her, thrusting her from it. She gracefully landed on her feet, rushing to grab her clothes and get dressed.

Once she was finished, she called Chaos through the bond. She needed to go to the northern village—to see the *Schatten*. There were several in the southern village now with the threats upon them, but there were a couple in particular she wanted to see.

If Elysia planned to sneak into Arcadia to spy on the enemy, she would need someone with her who had the expertise required for such a mission. Luckily for her, she had just the two for the job.

CHAPTER TEN

C athillian leaned over to Amelia and quietly asked, "How many is that?"

Amelia laughed. "Uh, well, my mind isn't the most reliable at the moment, but I think that's four shots of the hard stuff, and she just finished her fourth beer. But it's rearick beer, so it's stronger than any other kind of ale."

Cathillian hissed. "Yeah, *that's* gonna hurt in the morning."

"The betterrr question, 'thillian," Arryn slurred, "is why aren't *you* drinkin'?"

He laughed and lifted his own mug of brew. "I have been, dear. You just haven't noticed. You've been too wrapped up."

She eyed him suspiciously before holding out her hand. "Gimme the mug. I'm bettin' there ain't nothin' innit."

With a shake of his head and a smile, Cathillian handed her the mug. "See? It's half-full."

Arryn looked into the mug the same way she had looked at him a moment ago—suspiciously. "No," she said, shaking her head, "there's nothin' innit."

Cathillian opened his mouth to argue, but she tipped the mug back and drained its contents before handing it back to him, using her free arm to wipe the drips from her mouth and chin.

"See?" she said with a big smile. "It's empty."

Samuel slapped the table hard, howling in laughter as Arryn joined him. They leaned toward each other, laughing vigorously at the joke.

The rest of the table joined in, but not quite as heartily as Arryn and Samuel.

"That's my girl!" Samuel shouted, clapping Arryn on the back. He shoved a fist into the air. "Another round!"

"I want another shot," Celine said, lifting her hand as well.

"That's the spirit!" Samuel said. He looked at Cathillian. "These girls beat our arses taday on the battlefield, lad. Don't let 'em beat ye in drink, too."

"*Pffft.*" Arryn made the noise and got another round of laughter. "*He* told *you*!"

Cathillian narrowed his eyes as he leaned toward her, putting his mouth next to her ear. "Try standing. Let's see if I can beat you at that."

Arryn jerked away, giving him an evil look which he met with amusement. "Dick."

A drunk rearick woman stumbled across the bar, finding a seat on Samuel's lap. Arryn's eyes widened as she looked at him, giggling at his shocked "What the hell is happening right now, and what can I do to stop it?" expression.

"Lass, what's yer name?" the woman asked.

Arryn opened her mouth to speak, but a healthy belch came out instead. Her eyes widened as her hands clapped over her mouth. The woman in front of her, as well as the rest of the girls at the table, lifted their hands in a cheer.

Arryn laughed. "Sorry 'bout that." She shook her head a bit. "Arryn's the name."

"Hey," Samuel chimed in. "I dunno who ye are, but yer arse is diggin' inta me leg. Up with ye."

Using the table for support, the drunk rearick woman stood, ignoring Samuel as if he really *were* a chair.

"Ye should fight me," the woman offered.

Cathillian's eyes widened, but Arryn only smiled. "Hell, yeah! Now I'm oneofem!" she said, her words blending together.

"I figger if ye can drink with ol' Sam here, ye might be able ta fight, too," the woman said.

"Who *are* you?" Samuel asked, a confused grimace on his face.

The lady rearick turned, her hands on her hips and a knowing expression on her face. The moment she did, "ol' Sam" turned white as a ghost.

"Ah, ye 'member me now, ye old goat?" she asked.

He nodded, a sigh escaping him. "I remember, ye succubus. Get outta here."

The whole table laughed hard. "An old girlfriend of yours?" Celine asked with amusement.

Arryn had never before seen the shade of red Samuel's cheeks turned right then, and his eyes dropped to the floor.

The rearick woman laughed. "Sally's the name, but everyone calls me Sal. 'Girlfriend' is a bit strong of a word there, lass. Sam here got a wee bit shit-faced and wound up in me bed."

"Eh, shut it, *Salamander*. Go pester another table," Samuel spat. He shifted uncomfortably in his chair, avoiding eye contact with anyone.

Arryn knew Samuel had a thing for Celine, whether or not he wanted to admit it. Recognizing the silent call for help, even in her drunken haze, she decided to save her friend.

Arryn jumped up, immediately regretting the decision as the room began to spin even faster than it had a second before. "Sal! How about that fight? Let's go outside."

"Outside?" the woman said, laughing hard.

Without warning Sal threw a right hook, hitting Arryn straight in the jaw and knocking her off-balance. She hit the floor —after hitting several chairs on the way down—with a loud *oof*!

The bar cheered, everyone immediately drawn to the brawl. Cathillian and the rest of their table jumped to their feet, concerned about their highly intoxicated friend on the floor.

Reaching up, Arryn wiped blood away from her mouth. As she looked at it, she smiled.

"That fancy footwork ye have won't work in here, lass," Samuel said. "Things're different."

Arryn looked from the blood on her hand to the opponent smiling down at her. "*Fun.*"

Arryn climbed to her feet, using whatever she could for balance as she squared her stance. She raised her fists in front of her face for protection, and judged her opponent.

She'd had enough of real fighting and training. This was for fun, and nothing else. Everything had excited her lately. Going out on another adventure. The thrill of battle. The plan to get drunk and let loose in a town she had never been in. And now, a bar brawl with a seemingly friendly woman she had never met.

Sal threw another punch, but this time Arryn dodged to the right, throwing a punch of her own into the rearick's ribs. The woman stumbled back a few steps, and Arryn smiled darkly as she dropped her hands.

She heard Cathillian shouting something about getting them back up, but she didn't care. That wasn't the plan.

Without a care for being inside or any of the people standing around, Arryn charged the woman, plowing her shoulder into the woman's stomach and wrapping her arms around her as she lifted her and tackled her onto a table several feet behind her.

Glasses flew everywhere, shattering as the table broke under their weight. Both women hit the floor.

Arryn took another punch to the face before throwing her head forward and breaking the rearick woman's nose.

Samuel cheered and began taking bets on "the skinny one." Of course, no native in the bar other than Samuel bet against Sally, but that was what he had hoped for.

The women rolled around and threw punches every so often before separating and climbing to their feet. Arryn turned and grabbed a chair when she saw Sal reach for a mug.

Arryn swung, narrowly missing a patron watching from the sidelines before smashing it into Sal's side. The rearick dropped the bottle and collapsed to her knees. Arryn rushed over and lifted her fist, punching the woman hard and slipping on part of the chair she had just broken.

Landing hard on the woman, Arryn thrust her forearm in the rearick's throat, pinning her down to the floor.

"Relent," Arryn said.

The woman tried to move, but between the effects of the alcohol and the fight itself she didn't have the energy. Finally, she nodded, and Arryn collapsed next to her.

"The skinny one wins!" Samuel cheered.

There were mixed reviews, though everyone seemed impressed. Arryn and Sal looked at one another, and as soon as their eyes met, they began laughing. After struggling to roll onto her stomach, Arryn slowly climbed to her feet and helped Sal up.

"We need another round," Sally said.

Arryn laughed. "All I can taste is my own blood. I think it's time for me to quit."

"Ah, so soon?" Samuel said. "But we were just gettin' started, and everyone else is payin' now that I have their coin." He laughed at that last bit.

Cathillian looked at him incredulously. "Just getting started?" He pointed at Arryn. "Have you looked at her?"

"Is he always that whiny?" Sal asked.

Arryn laughed.

"*Hey*," Cathillian said, his voice showing the offense he had taken. "I'm *not* whiny. I'm just tired. We had a long day, and…"

"Yep," Sal said. "Definitely whiny."

Arryn only laughed again. "Don't be upset. But ya do sound a bit grrrouchy. You've been parental all night."

Cathillian shook his head and smiled. "When did I become the adult between the two of us?"

Arryn's brows lifted as she shrugged, her hands rising at her sides. "I dunno. Prolly the minnnute we crossed that threshold." She looked around. "So, hey. I'm bout to puke 'r pass out. I need a place to lie down."

Samuel chuckled. "Well, let's pay and get ye outta here."

"Ya know," Arryn said. "I'm not even sure I can make it wherrrever yer talkin' about."

"Shit. She's really fucked up," Cathillian said. "She's starting to sound like you, Samuel."

"Where'd ye think we picked up the accent, lad?" Samuel looked at Arryn. "All right, I'll talk to the 'keep. See if ye can stay here the night."

"After ye destroyed the place?" one of the barmaids said from behind them.

Samuel shook a bag of coins. "I can pay fer it. It just so happens I've recently come into some money."

The barmaid rolled her eyes. "Fine. She can stay."

Samuel bowed, handing the woman the bag of coins before she walked away.

"I can't believe you parted with your earnings," Amelia said.

Samuel smiled, shaking another pouch he had hidden on his belt. "It was a *really* good bet. The girl's a real cash cow—no offense."

Arryn gave a lazy, limp wave of her hand. "Nonnne taken. How 'bout that bed, hmm?"

She stumbled, but Cathillian caught her, immediately picking her up in his arms. Sal came by, nursing her swollen face with a wet cloth.

"Ye did good, lass. Ye can drink with me anytime," Sal said.

Arryn smiled. "Thanks. I might come back sometime and take ya up on that."

"Come on, my little adventurer. You've had a bit too much for one night," Cathillian said. "But you did pretty well adapting to the rearick brawl-style fight. Good job." He winked.

She smiled, snuggling into his chest before losing consciousness.

CHAPTER ELEVEN

P ain.
　　So. Much. Pain.

"Dear fucking goddess," Arryn groaned as she awoke to the sun blaring through a suddenly open window. It felt as though her eyes would explode. "Fuck, me. Would you turn that bitch off, please?"

There was a laugh from Cathillian. "What? The sun?"

Arryn groaned again as she rolled over and buried her face in her pillows, dragging the blanket over her head. "Yes! The sun. Make it go away."

"Someone drank too much. Come on, it's time to get up. They're kicking you out of the inn. It's well after noon."

Shocked, Arryn threw back the blankets and looked at Cathillian, but regretted it as soon as she realized the sun hadn't gone anywhere. Desperation filled her. Her stomach was roiling, and she knew she would throw up soon. She would need to be able to see to get outside, but Cathillian seemed too amused with himself to close the damned curtains.

The taste of bile hit the back of her throat as her adrenaline kicked in, urging her to move quickly or regret the consequences. She just needed a few more seconds…

"Are you serious right now? That's just cheating," Cathillian said.

The sun no longer a concern, Arryn jumped out of bed. Running to the window, she forced it open before hanging her head out and throwing up from the second story.

The sky was dark, her magic having responded to her shaky control well enough so the thick, dark clouds had formed overhead to shield her from the bright sun.

"So, uh…" Cathillian began, leaning against the wall just next to the window. "Abuse your power much?"

Arryn shook her head, restraining the urge to punch him because her stomach was fighting her again. "Shut it." Her voice was low and forced.

"My question is, why did you conjure clouds instead of healing yourself of the sickness?"

Arryn pulled back just enough he could see her and shot him an angry look, but it faded when she realized she really *had* just taken the harder road. Her shoulders slumped.

"Because I couldn't think straight. Bitch, this sucks," she said.

He laughed. "Being a druid has its benefits, sweets. You get to nearly kill yourself drinking if you want and feel no hangover. Though, I would imagine with how sick you feel, that cloud coverage probably depleted ya pretty good, didn't it?"

She groaned before pulling her head back in through the window and limply falling to the floor.

"*Uhhh,* make it go *away,*" she pleaded.

He stood there, looking down at her from his position leaning against the wall, his feet crossed at the ankles and arms crossed over his chest, smiling and shaking his head. "I have half a mind to let you suffer through this."

"Oh, *please,*" she said with a sarcastic tone. "You only have half a mind as it is. Now do me a favor? If I heal myself I'll have to take a nap—that's how pathetic I am right now."

Even with the pain she was in, she couldn't help but find her situation humorous. She knew why Cathillian was being stubborn. She had fought hard the day before; they all had. She had needed a good rest, but instead she had chosen to stay up all night drinking with the rearick—not something that was wise under even the best of physical conditions.

On the way into Craigston, Arryn had fallen asleep and nearly slid off the back of her tiger several times, though Samuel had only had to intervene once. A nice, warm bed was what she had been most excited to reach, but when she thought of being in a new place with new people—*good* people, those that could be *trusted*—she just couldn't help it. She had wanted to let go.

In the Dark Forest, she constantly felt the twin pressures of the imminent danger from Arcadia and from the dark druids down south. It was hard for her to forget those. But here, where no one knew who she was and no one other than the people most important to her knew *where* she was, everything felt safe. Warm.

She felt comfortable.

It was exactly what she had needed, even if she was paying for it in the worst way just now. Truth be told, she probably would have handled it better if she'd had more practice being sick. Without that experience, any ache or pain from illness seemed like a death sentence.

"Pleeeease," she begged. "I wanna be productive today."

Cathillian laughed. "A favor, huh?" he asked, mischief in his voice.

"Oh, no. What do you want?" she asked.

"Better not ask him that," Amelia said from the door. "Cathillian, I thought I told you not to torture her this morning."

"Hey! We both know she'd do it to *me*. I just couldn't help myself," Cathillian replied.

Cathillian leaned down, gently placing his hand on her cheek. *He felt so warm.* Had she been cold?

He gave a smile and whispered, "You owe me, baby druid," before his jade green eyes flashed brighter, his magic pulsing through her body and reviving her.

Within seconds, the headache, light and sound sensitivity, and her roiling nausea were all gone, only the memory of each left to torture her. His thumb stroked her cheekbone just under her eye before he winked and pulled away.

Arryn took the hand Cathillian extended for help and jumped to her feet, feeling much better than she had moments before.

"So, what are we getting into today?" Arryn asked.

"We all decided to take today and tonight to just relax," Amelia told her.

"Echo joined us, and she confirms the dark druids really *have* headed west. She says they are moving slowly," Cathillian said.

Amelia nodded. "Tomorrow morning, we'll head up to the Heights. Samuel and Celine will be staying here in Craigston. It's one hell of a climb, but it will be much easier after a full day and night of relaxing. Besides, I think you could use it."

Arryn quirked a brow before nodding. "I suppose you're right."

"I'm going to go tell Samuel you're once again part of the living," Cathillian said with a pat to her back. "Come down whenever you're ready."

She nodded and smiled. "Thanks. For healing me, I mean."

He paused a moment before nodding again and leaving the room. Amelia's eyes followed his every movement before she lifted a graceful hand and flicked her wrist, the door shutting after Cathillian was long gone.

Arryn's brows creased as she looked at the woman in confusion. "Is there a problem?"

Amelia looked at her knowingly. "Not at all. You don't remember our conversation from last night, do you?"

Arryn looked at her in deeper confusion. "I can't say that I do."

Laughing, Amelia rubbed her hands together like she was hatching an evil plan. "*Oh*, this is too good. Sit down. You're going to need to."

Nervousness began to fill Arryn as she sat on the edge of the bed. "You're freaking me out."

As Amelia sat next to her, her eyes flashed white. "I'm not going to tell you. You'll see it for yourself."

There wasn't enough time for Arryn to ask what she was talking about before images started slamming into her mind. It was obvious Amelia had been working to broaden her talents.

This was a new ability, but it was still rough, to say the least. Instead of a steading flow of imagery that swept through her mind like it was being seen firsthand, it was like these images were being thrown at her.

Though her technique needed work, Arryn tried to relax into it and allow them to tell her a story.

After the group had dropped off the injured to whatever doctors the rearick had, they had moved on to the bar. Despite her earlier excitement about the idea of letting go, Arryn remembered being concerned and wanting to stay behind.

Samuel and Cathillian had convinced her that rearick weren't a particularly sentimental bunch who celebrated battle. They celebrated those who died, and they celebrated surviving. In pain or not, the injured would want her to go have a drink for them.

And she'd had several.

Before going inside, she had cleaned her face, hands, and arms of the blood from the afternoon's battle. It wasn't perfect, but it would do. She had planned to get good and drunk enough to forget it. All those things, Arryn now remembered. The memories were hazy from exhaustion, but she remembered them.

It was what had come *after* the bar that was all new.

Cathillian had carried her outside, passed out from exhaustion, drink, and a few punches to the head. Ophelia's didn't have a shower, so Samuel told Cathillian where to find a local pond. It wasn't the lake behind his house that he had mentioned previously, but it would certainly do.

These images were all from Cathillian's point of view, so it was obvious that Amelia had been snooping around in his mind. She must have wanted to get even better acquainted with her gifts because of what was to come.

Arryn guessed she couldn't be angry at that, though she didn't like being a test subject when it was *her* mind being tampered with.

Not long ago—though it seemed like an eternity now—Cathillian had taken Arryn to the Kalt River to wash the blood and filth off her after she'd had her ass kicked by Nika, despite Arryn's winning.

This was no different. He slowly stepped into the water, fighting the chill of the water and his deepest wishes that it was warmer. She had been his only concern.

As he waded in, the cold water hit Arryn, causing her to stir uncomfortably. Though he was drained from pulling men out of the battle and healing them enough to save them from death, he couldn't help but use the last bit of magical energy he had to take the edge off for her. It was all he had left, but he gave it.

It hadn't been enough to take the effects of the alcohol away, or even the headache from being punched in the head several times, and certainly not her fatigue, but it had been enough to heal her broken nose, hand, and rib—all injuries she hadn't really felt due to the intoxication.

Her eyes slowly fluttered open as he began washing the surprising amount of blood and dirt out of her hair and doing his best to scrub it out of her clothes while she still wore them.

"What's going on?" she had asked as he ran his fingers through her hair.

He smiled. "You needed rinsed off before you would be allowed to stay at Ophelia's. Samuel said you probably couldn't make it back to his place tonight in your condition, so I came out here to help clean you up while Amelia and Celine secure and ready your room for you."

Arryn moaned in reply, a stupid, drunken smile on her face. "Thank you."

He smiled in return. "You're welcome." There was a pause as he continued to care for her before he finally spoke again. "I know we give each other a hard time. We pick on each other all the time, but you've always been there for me."

Arryn snorted. "I'm terrible to you. You know that."

There was a smile on his face, but it wasn't his usual "I don't take anything seriously" smile. It was something else. "I'm just as rotten to you. It's just us—we like to laugh. But at the end of the day, I know you're always there. Every time I broke something in training, it was you who nursed me until someone could heal me. When you started to get better at it, you would heal me yourself. You cared for me when I was in a coma for a few days after Jenna death-touched me, too. Even with the training continuing, even working at the Academy—you watched over me and made sure I was taken care of when you couldn't."

As she viewed Amelia's crudely formed images, she smiled, realizing he was right. She had always been the first to help him. Of course, she had also been the first to insult him and give him a hard time, too. But he had done the same for her.

Without ever asking, she knew that if she ever felt scared or worried she could go to him, and he would be there to make sure whatever hurt her paid for it. But she had always just assumed that was because they were raised as best friends. Druids were family, no matter what.

But she could sense his emotions through the way he looked at her, and the tone of his voice.

This wasn't just friendship.

"Amelia, I don't like this. This is an invasion of his privacy," she said.

CANDY CRUM & MICHAEL ANDERLE

"Why do you think that?" Amelia smiled.

"Because this is all through his eyes. I know everyone makes jokes behind our backs, but it's just not like that between us. And if it is from him, it's not fair that—"

"Stop," Amelia said. "Just watch. You're missing something. It's not an invasion of *his* privacy anymore."

Arryn quit fighting and once again let curiosity get the better of her. When Amelia began again, Arryn realized what she had meant. She somehow hadn't noticed when it had moved from Cathillian's point of view to hers, but it had.

It hadn't been his emotions she had been sensing, but her own as she looked into his sincere face and listened to his words.

"We've always been there for each other," he said. "I want you to know that no matter what, I always will be."

Arryn jumped up from the bed, her hands flailing around and her eyes wide as she cried, "Oh, goddess! Oh, *Bitch!*"

She looked back at Amelia, who wore a knowing smile as her eyes returned to their original color.

"See?" Amelia said.

"*Why?*" Arryn asked. "*Why* would you show me that?"

The image came back with fervor. As Arryn had listened to Cathillian tell her that he would always be there for her, her drunken mind had pushed away all hesitation and worry. Without warning, Arryn had thrown herself forward and kissed him.

She had kissed Cathillian.

Her arms had wrapped around him, and he had frozen there in the water, unsure of what to do. Then, he quickly melted into the kiss, returning it with just as much passion as she put into it.

"Please... *Please* tell me that was all that happened," Arryn pleaded.

Amelia laughed as she stood. "Yes, child. No worries."

Arryn's hands went to the sides of her head as she shook it, her eyes wide. "Elysia calls me that when I'm overreacting." Her eyes widened. "Oh, fuck… *Elysia*."

Amelia rolled her eyes. "There's a reason we all make jokes behind your back, you know. Do I look surprised this happened? You two fight like cats and dogs. You are both constantly picking on one another, but he was a *mess* without you. This was bound to happen at some point."

It was all a bit too much for Arryn. She didn't quite know what to think. "I feel terrible. I was drunk. I shouldn't have done that. I didn't even remember it! Oh, *Bitch*. That would be like a punch in the gut. Kiss someone and have them not even remember it?" Arryn's face turned deadly serious. "Wait. Can you like… pull that memory out of him?"

Amelia's eyes widened. "Arryn! No! Not only do I have *zero* clue how to do it and lack even a *fraction* of the skill to learn how yet, but that would be pretty shitty to do."

Heavily sighing, Arryn agreed, "You're right. Ugh. Okay. Well, I guess I'll just ignore it. Pretend I don't know. I am *not* ready to have that conversation yet. No way. I don't even think what you showed me was accurate. I mean, I felt *something* there, but I was drunk and vulnerable. That was probably all it was, so I'm not going to worry about it right now. There are way too many other things to focus on."

Rolling her eyes again, Amelia said, "Yeah, that's the answer."

Arryn's brows creased as she looked at her. "You know, you're getting *really* good at being a sarcastic ass."

"Be careful picking on me like that. I might think you're falling for me, too," Amelia quipped.

"Oh! You… I…" Arryn was so flustered she couldn't speak.

Amelia laughed. "Calm down before you explode. It was a joke. I'm not going to say a word about you knowing. Really, it's none of my business. *But…* When he carried you back in, you were asleep again, and his mind was practically screaming about what had happened. I thought you should know."

"Lemme guess," Arryn began. "You picked out my point of view while it was fresh in my sleeping mind."

Amelia smiled and nodded. "I was curious, okay? Besides, I needed the practice. You were so drunk I could only pick out rough pieces, because you were already starting to forget."

"I'm never drinking again," Arryn said.

Laughing, Amelia said, "I thought you'd feel that way. Now, come on. Let's go before Cathillian starts to suspect us."

Arryn wasn't exactly sure how she would keep her mouth shut on this one, but it needed to be done. While she'd had suspicions, not only about her own heart, but of Cathillian's as well for quite some time, it was neither the time nor place to be thinking that way.

They were on the cusp of war with Arcadia. By now the whole city would be against her. And once that was over, she was sure the dark druids would need to be dealt with.

If the Chieftain was right, they were moving west to get reinforcements. *No.* Forgetting her responsibilities and trying to be a normal girl at this moment would be a terrible decision.

Lives were on the line, and *she was no ordinary girl.*

CHAPTER TWELVE

I t was unusual for Alaric to leave his carved-out section of the
Dark Forest. That small piece by the caves along the very
edge of the mountains had been far enough away from Alexander
—that *so-called Chieftain*—and his daughter Elysia.

Neither the trees nor the animals surrounding their great
barrier had warned the druids of Alaric's presence. It had gone
unnoticed for many years. He had built a home for himself and
his people, and they had fed on the land, growing what they
could, but mainly surviving on the Forest.

As they traveled, the darkness and desperation of their old
home had slowly faded as the grass grew thicker and greener and
the trunks of the trees became sturdier and had more color.

They had exited the Forest directly to the west, and now
moved through the Terresian Plains. It was flat and vibrant
green, as green as the innermost parts of the Dark Forest where
Alexander and his lot of assholes were.

It was beautiful.

Contrary to the popular belief of the druids of the Dark
Forest, the dark chieftain didn't enjoy living among dead things.

It was simply the form his magic had taken, though his people had admittedly lost their way much more than he had.

He could still bring life, but he was far more capable of taking it.

Alaric was just as dangerous as Alexander, only his magic was the polar opposite.

"Chieftain," Aeris called as he approached. "It's getting late in the day. Should we find water and do some fishing?"

The dark chieftain smiled. "That will take too long. I'll feed the people."

Alaric lifted his staff, not speaking, but rather simply demanding obedience. His people slowed to a stop, awaiting his next move.

He lowered his staff, walking farther ahead as he turned to the west. Feet bare in the thick, lush grass, he thrust it into the ground just in front of him and his hollow eyes flashed with the faintest hint of green.

He pushed his magic outward and felt around the area, quickly finding what he sought. Soon, the sounds of thunderous hoofbeats echoed across the plain and several Highland cattle, large and thick with long fur and massive horns, came into view.

He could see young Aeris standing just off to the side, his wide eyes shifting between the cattle and back to his chieftain.

If it was a show he wanted, a show he would receive.

Once the cattle were close enough, the dark chieftain released a blast of power, forcing them into submission. He had seen his people use this technique, but they were quite pathetic at it.

Overwhelmed by his strength, the cattle came to an abrupt stop not twenty feet ahead of him, crying out as their legs began to shake. The dark chieftain could feel the pain emanating from them as he pulled his magic back, slowly draining the life from them.

When he had them where he wanted them, he thrust a hand forward and roots from a nearby tree burst from the ground, whipping upward as they splintered and delivered a death blow to each one.

Alaric dropped his hand, turning only his head to look at a shocked Aeris as his eyes faded back to normal.

"Dinner," was all Alaric said before lifting his staff from the ground and walking away, hoping his people didn't notice the look of intense fatigue in his eyes.

———

As the sun began to set on the Dark Forest, the governor, Nathaniel, and their warrior escorts, Cassondra, Ryel, and Clara, crossed the barrier into the druids' territory.

Relief flooded through the governor now that they were safe. The rest of the trip back had been slow, but uneventful. As the druids had expected, the remnant had been smart enough not to engage or follow.

Suddenly, with everything settled and no need to continue looking over his shoulder, the silence became deafening for the governor.

"So, Cassondra, are you married? Do you have any children?" the governor asked.

She smiled, her teeth a brilliant white against her healthy, glowing dark skin. "We don't marry like you outsiders, but we do have a ceremony of sorts. So, yes, I am 'married,' I guess you would say. We have a daughter. Rose."

The governor smiled. He wasn't surprised. Cassondra was beautiful. High cheekbones, a small nose with defined curves, full lips, and a heart-shaped face. Aside from her beauty, she was a strong warrior and very intelligent.

"He's a very lucky man. Is he a warrior, too?" he asked.

She nodded. "He is. Our daughter, she's fifteen and wants to be a *Schatten*. We couldn't be prouder."

His eyes widened. "Fifteen? How old are *you*?"

Cassondra laughed as she met his shocked gaze. "I am just shy of forty. My husband, as you would call him, is nearly fifty."

"Holy shit. I thought you were pushing twenty-five. Do you just have good genetics, or is that a druid thing?"

"You've met Elysia, yes? She and I are close in age. She's just over forty."

He lifted his eyes for a moment as he thought that over. "I suppose that makes sense. Cathillian is about twenty, I think they said, so her age makes sense. That also answers my question." He shook his head as he smiled.

As he turned to her, he opened his mouth and said, "Druid thing," at the same time she did.

They laughed.

"Clara," the governor called. "You are incredibly quiet. What about you and Ryel? Either of you married or have kids?"

"Clara is mute," Ryel replied from where he was riding behind them.

The governor's eyes widened as he struggled to look at them, horror on his face for having been so careless.

Clara's shoulders began to move as she burst into a silent laughter.

Ryel joined in as well. "Don't worry about it, Governor. She was born this way. We believe it makes her unique. She was born with a condition no one else here has, so she is special among us. She communicates through thought."

Really, please don't worry about it. The governor's eyes widened again as he heard a soft and kind voice flutter through his mind.

"You're able to use mental magic?" he asked Clara.

She nodded. *It isn't what you think, however. I don't look in the minds of others or create illusions. To me, nature magic is the only true and pure form of magic. It would be dangerous for me to be a warrior and unable to speak. In your world, I would be considered to have a disability. In reality, it just makes me better at my job. I'm more aware, and I'm also a lot quieter."* She winked and smiled.

"That's incredible!" he replied excitedly.

The group traveled the rest of the way to the village, chatting about anything and everything. It seemed the entire trip to this point had been filled with worry and anxiety, but once back in the safety of the Dark Forest, everyone felt just as relieved as he did.

The Chieftain came to greet them as they crossed into the southern village. He had been gathering everyone for their nightly fun.

"Ah! I see you've made it!" he said. "Welcome back, everyone. How was the journey?"

The governor exchanged looks with his druid companions and his son before turning back to the Chieftain. "I guess you could say it didn't go well."

The Chieftain's brows lifted. "That sounds like an interesting story. Come. We'll talk about it over some wine."

The governor smiled, knowing the Chieftain loved his wine at night and his kaffe in the morning. They were his favorites.

Once the mugs of wine had been handed out, the Chieftain wanted answers.

"So, in other words," he began after hearing the story, "you left them good and pissed off."

The governor sighed and nodded. "Yes. We did. It certainly hadn't been my intention, but it was obvious they came there for a fight. I'm betting that even if I *had* delivered Talia, they would still have wanted blood. They had decided on the way that they would have it whether they got what they were after with Talia or not."

Nodding, the Chieftain said, "I'd have to agree with that. What will you do now?"

"They've more than likely sacked the city by now," Nathaniel said. "Cella was abandoned, and there was no one to stop them. To get even, they probably burned it to the ground."

The Chieftain shook his head. "Not necessarily. If you weren't there to see them do it—for them to torture you directly with their actions—it's possible they left it alone. They like death and dismemberment. They like to make their victims' final moments twisted and painful, emotionally *and* physically. Torching the city after you left would have served no purpose. However, there's no way for me to know that for sure."

The governor sighed. "I guess there's a sliver of hope, but I'm not counting on it. Oh, well. There's nothing we can do about it until Arcadia is back under control and we have the full strength of the Guard on our side."

Nathaniel nodded. "Right. We made a deal with Amelia, and she'll honor it. That just seems to be who she is. Let's not worry about it now. We helped Arcadia, and they'll help us, too."

"That's true," the governor said, nodding his head as he tried to force away the negative thoughts. He pulled his eyes from the ground back to the Chieftain. "Where's Elysia? I figured she'd be here to greet us."

The Chieftain smiled, but the expression was unreadable. It didn't look either amused or sarcastic, so the governor wasn't quite sure what to make of it.

"My daughter got a little drunk and went for a swim. During her sojourn in the frigid water, she decided it would be a good time to go sneak into Arcadia." His voice was flat. Apparently, the smile had been one of moderate annoyance.

The governor's eyes widened, and his weren't the only ones.

A shocked Cassondra stepped forward. "What? Why would she do that? That seems so reckless… not like her at all!"

"At first, I didn't think so either. I was beginning to wonder if maybe she wasn't having a breakdown of some kind. She'd had too much to drink, and she was talking about Liam, Cathillian's father, and a lot of other things. She was excitable about it all. Once I got her to calm down, everything made sense, though I'm still not as happy about it as she was," the Chieftain said.

"What about this makes sense?" Ryel inquired, worry and a

tinge of authority entering his voice as he became even more concerned for his fellow warrior and Elder.

The Chieftain sighed. "I know it doesn't sound like her, but I let her go because I felt it was what was needed. Cassondra, you were there for her when Liam was killed. You know she cried that night, then woke up the next morning and acted like nothing happened. She has done that every day since. She never wanted Cathillian to see her weakness. Now that he's gone... Now that Arryn's gone..."

Compassion crossed Cassondra's expression. "She's being hit with a wall of emotion she has no idea how to deal with."

The Chieftain nodded. "My daughter is strong... stronger than even *I* knew. As I said, at first, I thought she was going mad, but when she calmed down I knew what this was. I went through the same thing when her mother died, only for me it came much sooner. The kids are grown. They are out fighting a war, and she is stuck here waiting for another to take place. But at this moment, we are not in danger.

"Elysia felt like she was sitting here doing nothing. She hasn't set foot in Arcadia since she was a child, so she has *no* idea what conditions are there—what Arryn and Cat will walk into. She feels like she's sitting here twiddling her thumbs with a smile on her face while she sends her children into a trap. Knowing what that feels like, I understand. I allowed her to go."

Clara stepped forward, and the Chieftain smiled and nodded.

"Yes, Clara. I saw her before she left. She was with Alehah and Rae, and before you ask, very sober and determined. I haven't seen her so determined in a while."

There was a pause as he nodded again, Clara having said something else to him.

The Chieftain stepped forward, placing his hands on her shoulders. "I assure you, she's just fine. The plan is for her and the *Schatten* warriors to sneak into the city. They are going to speak to the rodents and birds in the area, get trusted information. They want to know anything that might be of use to Cat and Arryn. No engaging, no warfare—just information. See? It's not so bad. This is giving her a sense of purpose, so I supported it, even if I don't like the risk. After all, these people do have mental abilities."

"We should all pray the goddess returns her safely," Ryel said. "All of them."

The Chieftain held his hands out to his sides. "Let's worry over this no more. Instead, let's celebrate your safe return! Always celebrate life—or death. How about some wine?"

The governor smiled. He hadn't had much experience with the druids, but he had learned two things: they were incredibly powerful, and the Chieftain used any excuse he could to "celebrate" with his people.

If he hadn't been responsible for an entire city, he might have considered a more permanent stay—that is, if they would have him.

CHAPTER THIRTEEN

A rryn silently stared at the impressive number of steps leading up the side of the mountain to the Temple of the Mystics, eyes wide. She swallowed hard.

"You ready?" Amelia asked.

Arryn looked at her, hope in her expression. "Is teleporting an option? Because I'm getting better, and I bet I can make it without excess fatigue."

With a roll of her eyes and a smile, Amelia said, "Nope. According to Julianne, when you make your first trip to the Temple, you must walk the whole way. If you cheat, you don't find any real enlightenment—or something like that. Anyway, it'll be my first trip, too, so we'll make it together."

Snow nudged her, a low purr rumbling in her throat as she silently offered to carry Arryn up the steps.

Taking a deep breath, Arryn nodded. "Okay, then. If we're gonna do it, may as well do it right." She turned to Snow and scratched her neck. "You and little man can just stroll with us. I'll make this hike myself, but thank you for offering."

Snow momentarily leaned into her touch before nodding and

pulling away. Arryn stumbled into Amelia as Dante darted through her legs to begin his run up the steps.

Amelia laughed as she helped Arryn stand upright again. "Well, *someone's* in a hurry."

She scowled at Cathillian with suspicion for a moment, hands on her hips, before turning back to Amelia. "That would be because *someone*, not to name any names"—she pointedly nodded her head in Cathillian's direction—"told Dante there would be a whole new group of people to snuggle him and tell him how damn precious he is. The cub is spoiled rotten already."

"Hey!" Cathillian said, poking a finger into her shoulder. "He might be bonded to you, but he's *my* best buddy. You shut your mouth. He's perfect."

Snow reached out and swatted Cathillian on the ass, shoving him forward as she growled.

"She said, 'You did this, so you get to deal with it.'"

His brows creased as he matched Arryn's defiant stance, hands on his hips. "I know what she said!" He turned to Snow. "And you might have birthed him, but he's my best buddy. You just shut your mouth, too! He *is* perfect."

Arryn rolled her eyes as Snow let out a louder growl, lunging at him a bit. Cathillian jumped and ran toward the steps. "I'm coming, Dante! The bitches are crazy!" he shouted, looking over his shoulder to make sure Snow wasn't really after him.

"Ha!" Arryn said, before laughing. "Serves him right. Nice one, Snow."

When Cathillian caught up with Dante, he snatched him up in his arms and hugged him tightly. Amelia, Arryn, and Snow began their walk up the steps. They had left Samuel and Celine back in the rearick town to tend to the house he hadn't seen in months.

It took quite some time to reach the top, and no one spoke as they fought the burn in their legs. Snow was the only one who didn't seem to be affected, and Arryn found herself regretting not taking the snow cat's offer.

After all, she had spent her entire life on a mountain. This was nothing to her.

When they reached the large entry doors, two men in robes awaited them. One had brown hair, while the other had dark auburn. Each wore a serious expression, but did not seem threatening—though Arryn knew they would be if challenged.

The moment they stopped, Arryn felt a familiar buzzing in her mind, the tingling feeling she had experienced often while teaching at the Academy. *It was the sensation of someone brushing against her mind.*

Amelia had given her brief lessons on how to shield her mind, but Arryn had no plans to do so now. If what Amelia had told her about the New Dawn was accurate, any attempt from her to shield herself would have been met with suspicion, and rightly so.

Besides, she had nothing to hide. In fact, the less she had to explain and the more they could learn from looking through her mind, the better.

The men looked at Snow with great concern, so Arryn took a step forward and ran fingers through her thick fur. The big cat purred before flopping down to the ground next to Dante—who was thankfully sitting still—and resting her large head on her paws.

"Greetings," the auburn-haired guard said. "My name is Nigel. Amelia, I know your face from Julianne. You are a near and dear friend to our Master."

Amelia stepped forward and smiled, bringing her hand to her head and then placing her fist over her heart, giving their salute of respect. The guard smiled and repeated the action.

"Thank you, Nigel. These are friends of mine. I'm unsure how much you saw in our minds, but Arcadia has been taken by a mystic—"

"Several," the dark-haired guard said, compassion in his expression. "I'm sorry for that correction, but there are several.

We have seen the images in the minds of the rearick coming and going from the city."

Amelia inhaled deeply, all happiness disappearing from her face. "I had suspected. We'd discussed the possibility, but there was no way for us to know for sure."

Nigel nodded. "Amelia this is Varick. Please forgive the lack of introduction. As for the news, I'm sorry. Your friends are wondering why we haven't made an attempt to stop it since we knew what was happening, but I think you understand."

Amelia looked at Arryn and Cathillian. "With the New Dawn pressing down on them, they are as trapped here as the Chieftain and Elysia are in the Dark Forest. Impending war."

"We have been lucky that the New Dawn have stayed away so far. We've recently received a visitor from beyond the Madlands, where Julianne has gone to deal with the threat. It seems she has been very successful so far. Still, we have to protect the Temple. Please, come in. You and your friends are welcome—even the furrier of you." He smiled at the tigers lying on the ground.

Amelia gave a polite smile and nodded. "Thank you, Nigel."

The guards led everyone inside. Arryn stayed very quiet, doing her best to push away the annoyance she felt at the constant buzzing in her mind. She didn't mind them being in her head, but she hated the sensation it caused.

After several moments, a warm, calming feeling washed over her. She felt her earlier discontent melt away, and she sighed. Comfort replaced any fear or worry from before.

"You're safe here, Arryn," Nigel said. "You've been through quite a lot, I see," he said, taking particular interest in her.

Arryn nodded. "You could definitely say that. I'm not exactly sure what you're referring to, though. I can't see what you looked at. I could only feel you looking."

"Oh! So, you're what we call a 'sensitive.' It means we can't snoop around in your mind without you knowing about it," he explained.

She nodded. "Before I ever had a clue what mental magic really was, I went to Arcadia and met Amelia. I almost immediately felt it when she nosed through my thoughts."

"Interesting. Do you practice? Sensitives usually make good mental magicians," he told her.

"Oh, no. I have my hands full enough with physical magic and nature magic. I don't need anything else. Amelia taught me enough that I can shield my mind. I don't really need more than that."

He chuckled. "There might come a day when that changes. If and when it does, feel free to come back. Before you leave, you should at least allow us to teach you how to properly meditate. In times of great stress, or when you have used too much magic and exhausted yourself, meditation can allow you to recharge without actually sleeping."

Now *that* sounded useful. "Thank you, I'd like that. I might not have need for illusions and things like that, but I can't deny the need for recharging on the go. I've been in several situations where that would've come in handy."

"The Frozen North?" he asked.

She looked at him, a bit surprised, then remembered he had been fishing around in her mind. She nodded. "Yes, the Frozen North. That mountain damn near killed me a few times, but I'm a lot stronger for it. I'll never regret it."

They wound through the halls, Amelia and Cathillian chatting with Varick as Arryn continued to talk with Nigel. Snow stayed close behind with Dante, looking at the tall walls and the art.

Though the tiger had been in the Arcadian Capitol building, there had been a sense of urgency the entire time, limiting her ability to look around. Arryn could feel her sense of wonder and excitement as they paced these halls.

They came to a great room with large dining tables. Nigel smiled as he gestured around. "Please, have a seat. We'll eat and have some drinks, and after that we'll discuss the things going on outside the Temple. I know your situation is urgent, but your stomachs are as well. It's necessary for a healthy mind!"

Varick's eyes turned white for a moment before he put his hands together and smiled. "We must get back to the entrance, but others will be in to welcome you. Zoe and Margit say they will be here soon."

With that said, Nigel and Varick helped them get comfortable before making their way out of the room.

"Julianne said they have great food here," Amelia offered, looking around the room.

"Given they live a life of indulgences to keep their *minds healthy*," Arryn replied, adding a bit of sarcasm to the last bit, "I'll bet the food will be pretty unforgettable. Speaking of which, my stomach is growling so loud I sound like Snow when she snores."

The tiger's gaze snapped to her, a low rumble in her throat.

"What? You're the only one who can make fun of people for snoring? You do, too, sweetheart."

Snow grumbled again, bumping into Arryn's chair and knocking it over. She spilled onto the floor, laughing as she relaxed there.

"You and Snow are *the* best friends I've ever seen," Cathillian said. He was holding Dante. "Not like me and my little buddy here at all. So much better."

"Oh, hush," Arryn said, standing. "She's just grumpy like her druid mom."

Cathillian opened his mouth to speak and Arryn held up her hand.

"Are you *really* going to walk into that?" Amelia asked Cathillian.

Laughing, he turned and sat down in a chair, adjusting the cub in his lap. "I guess not. I'll pass—this time."

Arryn fixed her chair and took a seat. "Thanks. I think they'd frown at murder on the Temple grounds."

Cathillian rolled his eyes and went back to snuggling Dante—

further spoiling him—while Amelia sat on the floor next to Snow, soon lying against her and using her as a pillow.

Arryn closed her eyes and tried to clear her mind. She wondered if meditation was anything like what she had always been taught to do. While she had no interest in learning mental magic, she would be excited to learn meditation. Thinking of what she had been through lately, she knew it could potentially save their lives.

CHAPTER FOURTEEN

E lysia, Alehah, and Rae made it to Arcadia just as the sun was going down. They stayed back, patiently waiting for the sun to finish setting and the city to go to sleep.

The plan was simple enough, and Elysia had full faith they could pull it off without getting caught, but there was always a chance. That was why she had brought the *Schatten* with her. They specialized in subtlety and would be a great help to her.

Her father had been concerned for her well-being, but in truth she hadn't felt so good in quite some time. The whole time Cathillian and Arryn were in Arcadia, she been sitting in trees as she watched the wall, or on patrol, or even fighting occasionally.

All the while wondering—worrying—what might be happening in Arcadia. Every note Cathillian had sent seemed quick. Straight to the point. He was always a terrible liar, and she had a feeling the letters weren't honest, though she had often wondered how much of that was her own suspicion and how much of it was guilt.

She had been lying in her letters to Cathillian, too. How many times had she told him everything was fine while they were being attacked or stalked from a distance by the dark druids?

Still, her worries about the possibility he and Arryn might be in trouble she had always kept to herself. The last thing she needed was to give her father even *more* reason to think she was overprotective.

As it turned out, however, she had been right. Arcadia *had* been in danger, and they had been right in the middle of it. Once Cathillian had returned to the Dark Forest, and she realized her bad feeling had been more than that, she had become even more determined to help.

While Arryn was gone, and they had no idea where, she had been stuck. They were *all* stuck—even Cathillian, who wanted to help more than anyone. It pained her to see so much hurt in his eyes, and more than once, she feared he had suffered the same fate she and his father had, only for Cat and Arryn it would have been before they had even had a chance to get started.

With not one, but *two* battles on the horizon, Elysia couldn't stand the thought of sitting by any longer. She needed to do something while the Dark Forest was temporarily safe. If she moved fast, she would have what she needed and be back before anyone really missed her.

"We should approach from the west," Rae said. "Not only is it in our direct path, but it's the least populated area in the city, it seems."

As they approached, Elysia focused her power as Rae had, sensing for life. She felt the presence of hundreds of small essences—those of the rodents in the tunnels below the city, as well as in the streets. She also felt the lives of those humans in the area—the shadow warrior had been right. There weren't nearly as many on this side.

Elysia nodded to Rae and Alehah, giving them the go-ahead. She would follow, and do her best to recreate their actions. She had always wanted to learn the ways of the *Schatten*—the shadow warriors—but she hadn't been patient when she was younger.

She certainly was now. It would be a good time to learn.

Rae stepped forward, her green eyes beginning to glow as the weak vines that naturally climbed the stone walls bloomed and spread out. Within moments, they had a sturdy ladder to climb to the top.

Elysia watched as the women scaled the wall at record speed, so quickly that she wasn't quite sure if they had even touched anything. But that was part of their strength—they spent their whole lives training in climbing and becoming faster than any of the other druids. They spent most of their time in the trees, and some of them even slept in their branches.

Elysia took a deep breath and ran forward, latching onto the ladder and climbing to the top, where the women patiently waited for her. They hung from the edge, and once she met them, they slowly pulled themselves up after sensing for any presence at the top.

They swung themselves over the stone railing and ducked down as they ran across the top of the wall, making sure to stay low enough not to be seen from below.

Several bats flew overhead, and Elysia's eyes flashed as she silently called them to her. One landed in her hand, and she held it as she spoke quietly.

"I need you and your friends to be our eyes. We are going to move through the city, and we can't waste all our power sensing people. Will you warn us if you see anyone?"

The bat squeaked in agreement and she let him go. The warriors gave the bats several moments. Then the *Schattens'* eyes flashed and thick vines sprouted and reached for them, wrapping around their waists before lowering them quietly to the ground below.

While Elysia was strong enough to do it herself, her magic wasn't nearly as quiet as theirs. The shadow warriors failed whole training exercises if their vines or anything else they cast were heard. Elysia's usually exploded free, causing enough noise to garner attention—especially in a hushed city.

Quietly, the three women made their way through the city, stopping and questioning rats and even snakes that came up from the tunnels upon their command. These were the creatures that could get anywhere.

"There are five of them," Elysia whispered. "That's not good. How the hell are Cat and Arryn supposed to take on *five* mystics?"

Rae sighed and shook her head. "I think they are in over their heads. Mystics don't fight like the rest of us. Fireballs and blasts of wind can be dodged if someone knows what they're doing. It's impossible to dodge a direct mental attack from a mystic."

Elysia nodded. "I've been lucky enough never to fight one, but my father has told me what they're capable of. Selah could take down men by overwhelming them with pain and suffering to the point they passed out, or he could just convince them they were so tired they could no longer stay awake."

Alehah looked around, keeping watch for a moment before joining in. "What if we take a couple out?"

Elysia's eyes widened. "What? No, we can't. I promised my father I wouldn't engage. This is a fact-finding mission only, and we have our facts. There are five of them, and the dead body of the one Arryn killed is being eaten in the sewers by our little friends. I say we stick to the plan."

Alehah knelt next to the other two. "If we do nothing, Arryn and Cathillian *will* advance on this place. They are seeking help right now, but if the Temple is in as much danger as the Arcadian Chancellor said, they won't send more than one, *maybe* two. How is he or she going to stack up against an army controlled by pure evil?"

Elysia was quiet for several seconds as she thought over Alehah's idea. It was terrible to even think of doing, but she couldn't deny the woman was right. Everything she had said was accurate. There were too many for a single mystic to help with, and what if they didn't part with any? What then?

Would *Amelia* be able to help?

Hell, no. She had only mediocre mystical skills at best, though Elysia applauded her will to learn the second form of magic. It had proven useful to her thus far, but it wouldn't be enough to take back a city.

Things needed to be evened out.

"You can't be serious," Rae said, staring her Elder down. "Are you *seriously* thinking about doing this?"

Elysia opened her mouth to speak, but it closed again. "I… Ugh. Look, she's right. If we go back, Arryn and Cathillian could decide to do the very thing we've done here, and get killed."

"Exactly!" Alehah said excitedly, still making sure to keep her voice a whisper. "Rae… Who better to do this than us? This is what we do—what we train for. This isn't battle. This will be an assassination."

Rae stared at her partner for a moment. "If we didn't have our Elder here with us, I wouldn't question it, but we were brought as insurance. We are here to make sure she comes home in one piece. Will you be the one to break the news that we lost her during an assassination attempt we'd promised wouldn't happen?"

Elysia waved a hand. "Hi, guys. Right here, ya know."

Alehah began to speak, but went silent again, her face turning serious as her eyes began to glow.

"We have company." Instead of speaking the words, she mouthed them.

Bats flew overhead, squeaking as they did. Elysia looked at her partners and nodded.

Rae grabbed her knife from the sheath on her thigh and leaned against the wall, somehow melding into the shadows. Alehah led Elysia behind one of the buildings they had been crouched between.

A guard walked around the corner, his magitech rifle raised as

125

he stepped into the alley. Everything went silent, and Elysia desperately wanted to know what was happening.

Then, Alehah stepped out, nodding toward Elysia. Her brows creased with confusion as she slowly looked around the corner. The guard was gone, and there wasn't a single trace of him anywhere.

"Uh…" Elysia said.

Rae pointed toward the roof, and Elysia looked. Somehow, Rae had taken the guard's life and moved him to the roof without a single sound being made.

Not one sound.

She had known the *Schatten* were good, but Rae was certainly among the best. "Wow," was all Elysia could manage.

Rae winked. "Thanks. Now, we have our information. We should leave."

Alehah stood in her way. "You're not going anywhere." The woman's voice was suddenly at normal volume, the pitch authoritative.

"Alehah! You *must* be quiet. We don't want to catch the attention of another guard," Elysia scolded.

The warrior's eyes narrowed as she looked toward Elysia, a wicked smile pulling at the corners of her mouth. "Oh, sweetheart. Those guards are the *last* thing you have to worry about."

Realization struck Elysia as she stared at her friend—the woman she was about to fight.

"She's under their control," Rae said, no longer caring about her volume either. "We'll incapacitate her and flee. Their control can only reach so far."

Alehah's hand was a blur as it pulled her knife free and threw it at Rae, the blade piercing her just under the sternum. Rae groaned in pain as she fell to her knees.

"Go!" Rae shouted. "Get out of here, Elysia!"

Elysia's eyes flashed dark green as she prepared for whatever might happen, the glow casting low light in the dark alley as power emanated from her. "I leave no one behind."

Heavy footsteps approached down the cobblestone road ahead, and Elysia took her chance. She charged for Alehah, ducking under an inexperienced blow. It was obvious that whatever mystic was controlling her didn't have nearly the training the warrior did. Whoever it was severely stunted the druid's abilities.

Stupid move on their part.

Elysia recoiled from ducking away only to came back at her friend and thrust a knee into her abdomen. Alehah doubled over, coughing as she tried to catch her breath.

"You'll forgive me later," Elysia said before grabbing a rock and smashing it over her head, dropping her to the ground.

"Good, now use the vines and get her over the wall," Rae said, her eyes glowing as she pulled the knife free and began to heal herself.

Just as Elysia had gotten Alehah's unconscious form back over the wall with the aid of the vines they had climbed over with, six guards rounded the corner. She turned to see Rae unleashing hell on them, but even with all her combat training she wasn't as fast or as good as Elysia.

Eyes still glowing, Elysia ran into the fight. Rae had already taken one down. Elysia jumped into the air and mule-kicked another in the chest, sending him flying into the road. She arched back, cushioning her landing on her hands and allowing her back to softly hit the ground before her legs swung forward, propelling her to her feet.

Crouching, Elysia struck, punching the next guard in the groin before delivering an uppercut to his chin. As he stumbled backward, she reached for her knife and slit his exposed throat open before turning and throwing it into the chest of the fourth.

Elysia watched as Rae took down the fifth with a kick to his knee before snapping his neck. She dropped to the ground, rolling out of the final guard's reach as she retrieved the knife from the chest of Elysia's kill before turning and throwing it, the guard falling to the ground with the blade sticking out of his throat.

Breathing hard, they retrieved their weapons before standing for a moment in the middle of the bodies.

Rae shook her head. "Something's not right. I can feel whoever it is trying to get in my head, but they can't."

Elysia nodded. "You have a natural resistance to mystical magic. I can feel it, too, but that's because my father taught me how to create a mental barrier. The Founder taught him."

"But I thought they could break through that," Rae said with obvious confusion, using the back of her arm to wipe blood from her face.

"No, you're right; something's not right. They normally *can* break past a block, especially novice ones like ours. This is a good sign. Whoever is doing this is fatigued. They are stretched as thin as they can go. Alehah must have been vulnerable."

Rae smiled darkly. "And now we know they are, too. They fucked with my favorite partner. I've changed my mind. I think I want mystic blood."

Elysia nodded. "We find this one, we get out. If we run into even an *ounce* of trouble…"

Rae nodded. "We flee."

The women called on their magic, vines lifting them to the rooftops as they cleared one after another. They put a call out to the owls and bats alike, asking for their help to locate the mystic. They were the ones who had seen them and knew what they looked like. It would be easy to find them.

Several rats scurried across the roofs with them, following as the women did their best to remain as silent as possible. When they reached the end of the block, they saw the barracks.

"Shit," Rae whispered. "If we get caught, we're fucked."

Elysia only nodded. "I guess we'd better be pretty quiet then, huh?"

Rae smiled briefly before it fell, and her eyes widened. Footsteps echoed all around them. Elysia's eyes quickly dropped to the street ahead of them to see almost a hundred guards flooding into the wide-open intersection.

"Shit," Elysia said, repeating Rae's earlier sentiment.

Elysia was about to suggest fleeing, but an owl flew over, calling out to them. *The mystic is in those barracks*, the owl told them. He had seen him run inside.

"We can't leave the roof," Elysia told the owl, watching the men below carefully.

The owl circled again, coming back to call out again.

Rae looked from the owl to Elysia. "Clearly he doesn't see what we do." The druid shook her head as she focused again.

Realization struck the druid Elder then. "That's because mystics can't affect the mind of animals. He doesn't see what we do because *it doesn't exist.*"

Rae's eyes widened. "But I thought... Barriers..." She was obviously confused.

Elysia smiled. "There are *two* of them in there, and they're working together to overpower us. I'm willing to bet the first one was in there and called for backup. The owl saw a man go in. They're *both* in the barracks."

The men ahead of them began to fade in and out as they saw the truth. No one was there.

Rae looked to the left and pointed. "There's a huge tree over there."

Elysia nodded, her eyes never leaving the barracks. "Let's rip them apart."

Running like hell across the roofs, Elysia and Rae made their way to the tree. As they climbed down, they felt through the ground and found its root system.

Barefoot, as they usually were in battle, they walked along the road, connecting with the earth below as their power traveled through their feet and into the roots.

The ground shook as the tree grew exponentially. They approached the barracks, and Elysia stepped forward, her eyes almost lighting the way. She saw white eyes staring back at her through the glass, and she could feel them struggling to gain control of her, but it was impossible.

Elysia could sense Rae's life essence behind her, shifting rapidly as she approached. The mystics couldn't assault the Elder, so they settled for the shadow warrior with the weaker barrier instead.

With a flick of her wrist, Elysia sent the wind after her. It hit the *Schatten* hard and began to spin in a small but powerful cyclone, just big enough to lift her from the ground and hold her there.

The mystics inside began to sweat as they lost their leverage.

Elysia smiled as she slowly lifted her hand out to the side. Then she swung it forward, the thick roots bursting from the ground and smashing into the side of the building.

The wall crumbled and trapped the mystics, who had been unable to run. Elysia sensed a large number of rats suddenly approaching—they had caught up to her.

The mystics struggled to move, but their legs were pinned. Elysia knew she couldn't waste any more power than she already had. She would need the rest to retreat from the city, and that would need to happen *soon* because the Guard would surely be on their way.

The barracks was empty, which meant the occupants of this particular building were out on patrol.

Elysia raised a finger and pointed to the terrified mystics in the building. "Dinner, boys and girls."

The mystics eyes faded to normal as they screamed and did all they could to pull the rubble from their legs, but it was too late. Rats descended upon them and other animals like bats and owls followed suit, quickly coming to understand what was being asked of them.

Elysia turned to her friend, quickly dropping the cyclone and running to her side. "Are you okay?"

Rae nodded. "I lost my damn breath in that thing!" she said, struggling to catch it now. "Any longer and I'd have choked to death!"

Elysia grimaced. "Sorry about that. We'll talk about it later. We need to go. *Now.*"

The women ran as fast as they could toward the wall, taking solace in knowing they had ended two of the mystics as their screams were abruptly cut off.

"Nice going with the rats," Rae said between breaths.

Elysia smiled. "Yeah, well, they were weakening anyway, but I didn't want to take any more chances. They can't control the animals, but I can."

They quickly climbed the wall and went over the other side. It didn't take long for them to find Alehah and heal her. Each of them was exhausted, but they managed one last run back to where they had left the horses, almost a mile away.

As Elysia climbed on Chaos' back, she realized just how big a mistake the trip had been. The trip itself had been a wonderful idea, and she had stood by her word. That being said, it was the argument over making an assassination attempt that had gotten them caught.

She had been so sure she was making the right decisions in there, and she had—until Alehah played on her emotions. The girl was young and had wanted to really test her abilities, she imagined.

That would be dealt with once they reached the safety of the Dark Forest's barrier.

Now, there were far larger problems. Elysia had just accidentally declared war on Arcadia.

CHAPTER FIFTEEN

Scarlett stood in her office, her expression unreadable as she stared at Nikolai and Barbara. The two mystics looked nervously at one another as they awaited their leader's next words.

"So, let me get this straight," Scarlett said, leaning back on her desk, crossing her arms over her chest and her legs at the ankles, and sighing as she looked at the ceiling. "Not only did that bitch make it into the city, but she managed to take out *two* of us?"

Nikolai cleared his throat. "Y-yes. That's what I'm saying. We checked the rubble, like you asked. We found them in the barracks that was destroyed."

Barbara scoffed. "Not that there was much left to find."

Scarlett's eyes shot daggers at Barbara, causing the lesser mystic's amused expression to fade immediately.

Taking a cautious step forward, Nikolai asked, "I don't mean to upset you further, but I must ask. Where were you? When the guards came for you, you weren't home. We've been trying to piece this together all night."

Scarlett turned her icy glare on Nikolai. "Oh, I was busy being productive. Someone around here has to be, unless you plan to do that by *dying*. Then I suppose that would be pretty fucking productive."

Both mystics wisely stood and kept their mouths shut as Scarlett sighed and shook her head. Her nostrils flared as she looked toward the window.

"For your fucking information, I was preparing for something just like this. I figured it wouldn't be long, though I didn't realize it would come this soon."

"Preparing?" Barbara risked. "How so?"

"Well, I tried to call in some reinforcements, but the dark druids proved to be a bust. I helped them out a while ago—retrieved that spoiled little brat and her parents they were after—and I expected a return on my loyalty. A messenger returned shortly after I did to tell me the dark druids are gone, but I have other plans."

She paused for a moment, taking a drink of her mystic's brew. "Luckily for me, I have friends all over. Lots of people owe me lots of favors. I called in a few. There will be several more mystics joining us, and a few unique physical magic users. We will need specialized magic if we want to win this. Something they've never seen."

At that moment, there was a knock at the door, and Scarlett waved her friends off to go answer it. The door opened, and a young man walked in. He seemed serious, but was not at all afraid.

"Good morning, Chancellor," the young guard said.

Scarlett turned on the charm, even pushing a bit of influence on him. He suddenly felt warm and welcome in her office, stunned by her beautiful smile.

"Good morning," Scarlett replied. "What brings you to my office?"

He smiled back, taking a step closer before turning serious again, no doubt remembering why he was there. "I'm sorry to report, Chancellor, that a scout who just returned says he saw

Amelia and Arryn a couple of days ago heading into the southern mountains—into Craigston, we think. He didn't engage. There were apparently several people in her group."

Scarlett nodded. "That was wise of him. He never would have made it out alive if he'd attacked. Now, because of his bravery, we have the report and know where she is."

Nikolai's brows creased. "But if she's in Craigston, how could she ha—"

"Thank you," Scarlett interrupted. "I appreciate this information. Please let me know if anything else comes up."

Without speaking, Scarlett pushed her influence on him again, giving him the sense that he should leave right away and help outside the office in whatever way he could. He smiled again, bowing his head before taking off.

As soon as the door closed, Scarlett's façade dropped, and she once again scowled. "You idiot. Seriously?"

Nikolai's eyes widened. "I'm sorry! What did I do?"

She sighed heavily. "It's obvious that Arryn wasn't the one who attacked the city. If she's in Craigston, that means she's going to the Temple for help. Got it?"

Realization struck him then. He nodded. "If she's at the Temple, Julianne might come back with her."

Scarlett waved a hand. "There's no worry of that. I have reports that Julianne is off in the Madlands somewhere, fighting the New Dawn. Still, there are a lot of people at the Temple that I wouldn't particularly care to run into."

"If I may," Barbara said, giving a wicked smile as she stepped forward. "We might be able to take advantage of this."

Tilting her head to the side with curiosity, Scarlett waved a hand for her to continue.

"Arryn and Amelia were headed into Craigston right after all those guards were killed. It shows she's not in the Dark Forest, and really does look like she's hiding out. How certain are you that it wasn't Arryn who attacked?"

Scarlett smiled. "Positive. You're all still alive."

Barbara and Nikolai looked at one another, and Scarlett could sense the dread they felt from that one statement.

"If it *had* been Arryn and Amelia, they would have brought several mystics—possibly with more power than us. Given they haven't expended their time and energy with compelling a city full of people, I'd have to say they would be *much* stronger." She took another drink of her brew.

Barbara smiled again. "The timing works. Arryn could have fled after the murders and made it to the southern mountains easily. It wouldn't take much to say she'd come back to do some more. We could call it an act of war."

Scarlett nodded. "Okay. And who are we going to declare it on? The Heights? Craigston? Because I'm pretty sure that even with the training going on around here, one rearick is worth several Guard. I don't care to go to war with either of those, not with Arryn and Amelia backing them up."

Shaking her head, Barbara said, "Not the Heights. Think about it… If Arryn is up there, where *isn't* she?"

Scarlett shrugged. "The Dark Forest. I would assume that is the point here."

"Exactly. If they aren't there, the Dark Forest has been left open."

Laughing, Scarlett said, "Yeah! Except for the hundreds of druids—including their Chieftain—who reside there. This sounds like a great plan."

Barbara sighed, not having considered the Chieftain. It was then that Nikolai seemed to get a bit more chipper. "What if we don't get close?"

"Explain," Scarlett demanded.

After thinking for several moments, Nikolai said, "What if we take physical magic users, Guard, and ourselves to the edge of the Dark Forest, where it's possible they won't sense us. Come on…

You've made the threat several times now. What if we actually *do* it?"

Scarlett's mouth fell open slightly as she realized what he was saying. "Burn it to the ground."

He nodded. "If we took horses and carts, we could transport oil. The physical magic users could open the barrels or gouge holes in them and levitate them over the trees, saturating them in it. After that, only a single fireball would do it."

"Yes!" Barbara chimed in. "They won't have Arryn or Amelia there to control the blaze, and if they call storms, the rain won't be able to put out the fire. It won't even be able to wash the oil off. They'd be fucked. The Forest would burn, no matter what."

Scarlett sat there for several moments, her mind exploding with ideas. Suddenly, this half-baked idea didn't sound too bad. In fact, it sounded perfect. If they took enough barrels of oil, they could do a lot of damage.

A smile spread across her face then as she nodded. "After all, they *did* just declare war on Arcadia. Not once, but twice. I think, since the Guard was on our side before, they won't have a problem with this. Still, we will have to wait for backup to arrive. We will need crowd control."

Barbara nodded. "We ourselves will have to go. There would be no way we could trust them if we didn't. Once they got close to the Dark Forest, their fear of the druids would be enough to snap them out of the compulsion unless we were right there."

"I agree," Nikolai said. "There are a lot of weaker-minded people in this city who aren't actually being controlled at all. If they became too cowardly, they could flee and cause the others to do so as well, even if the compulsion holds. We will definitely have to go."

Scarlett shrugged. "It will be a show of good faith. Having the leader go and not be afraid of getting her hands dirty will look good to the people. Don't you think?"

Barbara nodded and smiled, obviously feeling a bit better

after the earlier bad news. "I think we have some work to do. We don't have a clue how long it'll be before Arryn gets back from the Heights, or who she will have with her."

Nodding, Scarlett said, "There's one more thing. We need to test the resolve of the people. Plus, it wouldn't hurt to weed out the traitors amongst them. I think it's time for some fun."

"How do you plan to do that?" Barbara asked.

"Oh, you'll see. I promise, it will be nothing short of entertaining. That being said, I think you should work on setting up a town meeting at the Capitol steps." The mystic winked as she moved to seat herself behind her desk.

Taking their cue, her loyal friends turned and headed for the door.

THE TEMPLE WAS INCREDIBLE—EVERYTHING Julianne had said it would be. Amelia sat with her legs folded in, her hands resting palm-up on her knees, and her eyes closed tightly, with Margit seated just in front of her. Arryn was positioned in the same manner, with Zoe in front of her.

"Do you realize just how tense your face looks when you're trying to meditate?" Margit asked Arryn.

"Shh," Zoe said. "She's *my* student. You have your own."

Amelia opened her eyes to see Margit pointing at Arryn. "Well, she looks like she's trying to shit. Good luck with that one."

Amelia bit her lip to stifle a laugh. She wasn't exactly sure how old Margit was—close to Ezekiel's age, she would imagine—and like the Founder she was incredibly feisty. She was the type of older woman who had worked hard and knew she had earned the right to say whatever she wanted.

Zoe, Arryn's instructor, was young, but had a fire of her own. Her tight, dark curls bounced as she turned angry brown eyes on Margit. "Hey! I don't care if she actually does shit her pants as long as I teach her something. You just wait. You'll see."

"See her shit her pants?" Margit asked, causing Amelia to laugh loudly.

Arryn raised her hand. "Hi. I'm right here. Also… *Not* gonna shit my pants."

Margit raised a brow. "You sure about that? You look positively constipated."

Amelia laughed again and Arryn shot her a look before glancing back at Margit. "Yep. Pretty sure. In fact, I'll tell you a little secret." Arryn leaned forward a bit, cupping one of her hands to the side of her mouth as she whispered, "I don't even need to."

Rolling her eyes, Margit returned to her neutral position and shook her head. "Your student is a smartass."

"Sure is. Julianne would love her." Zoe reached out and tapped Arryn's leg. "She's kinda right, though. You really do look stiff."

Still smiling, Amelia said, "Pretend you're sitting alone on the bank of the river. The trees are all around you, and the sun is shining on your shoulders. Imagine how good it feels, how relaxing it is. You don't have to *try* to meditate. It's supposed to be relaxing. That's how it lets you renew your strength."

Arryn shook her body, loosening herself up before she settled back in. "Okay, I'll try again." She took a deep breath and closed her eyes.

Satisfied, Amelia turned back to her own teacher, winked, and shut her eyes before relaxing back into the meditation. They had been at the Temple for a full day, after having spent the night. It was almost time to get back on the road to return to the Dark Forest, and Amelia was trying to pack all she could into the short visit.

When they had explained to Margit, who was in charge in Julianne's absence, what had happened and allowed her to see all what each of them had seen—including how easily Amelia had been manipulated—she had given permission for Zoe to return with them.

Amelia couldn't deny it would have been amazing to have both along on the trip. Someone with Margit's feisty personality and incredible skill would go a long way in the fight against the mystics, but she couldn't leave her people while there were dangers for them to face as well.

They were simply grateful the mystic had agreed to send even one. It would be quite the blessing to have Zoe along. Even though she was young, she was very strong and a master storyteller.

"Illusions are much different than looking into the mind," Margit said.

Arryn snorted. "No shit."

Margit sighed. "Are you commenting on something, dear? Or were you simply giving us an update on the contents of the seat of your pants?"

Amelia opened her left eye, fighting a smile as she turned toward her friend with the sarcastic attitude. Arryn gave a grand smile. "You mean to say, the *lack* of contents in the seat of my pants." She winked before closing her eyes again.

That girl never ceased to amuse Amelia. She and Cathillian were so much alike in that way.

We should talk in the privacy of our own minds, Margit sent telepathically. *While I find your friend amusing, she's obviously trying to cover up her difficulties with jokes.*

Amelia nodded, though her eyes were closed. *I'm not surprised. She has a lot of potential, but when things are uncomfortable for her, she jokes. She'll get it.*

I know she will, Margit sent back. *She's a smart girl. That being said, she isn't my student. You are. Now, as I was saying... Illusions are much different than looking into minds. When you're looking, you are simply opening your mind to another and accepting any information that comes your way. Useful things are usually on the surface and will*

*come to you freely if no blocks are in place, but you must push if you
need something more.*

"Uh..." Arryn said out loud. "I don't like this."

"Shh," Zoe said. "It's your mind opening to things around you.
The meditation is working."

"Nope. I don't like hearing someone else's thoughts. It's an
invasion of privacy," Arryn replied.

"You're hearing them because they have dropped their barriers," Zoe said. "If you heard Margit's instructions, then you know
what she just said is true. You opened your mind. Their conversation was just on the surface, so there wasn't a block to keep you
out. The information spilled out for you to hear. That isn't an
invasion of privacy. Hell, we rarely speak aloud around here. It
would be an invasion for you to dig farther. For you to bully your
way past a barrier. *That* we don't normally do."

"Though, sometimes that's necessary," Amelia added, then
turned her mind back to Margit.

"She's right. I saw what she had to do while you were in the
North. Had she not invaded the minds of others, she wouldn't
have known who to trust, and she would have been dead. We
normally respect the privacy of others—unless lives are at stake.
Would you prefer to be polite, or alive?" Zoe said.

Amelia could hear Arryn sigh, and she could feel her resolve
and understanding through her own hyperawareness from
meditating.

Arryn went silent as she gave in to the meditation and all it
offered, including the ability to read surface thoughts. When
Amelia had begun learning, it had taken her a while to get
that far.

But Arryn was different.

Not only was she incredibly strong both mentally and physically, but she knew two forms of magic already. When Amelia
had begun, she had only known physical magic. It was always
difficult to learn a second. But nature magic was incredibly spiri-

tual anyway. Mental magic would come easily to her if she chose to learn it, though Amelia understood why she didn't want to.

The mystics continued to speak in silence to their students as they gave them individual lessons that fit their own needs.

Amelia focused as she sat with Margit, paying close attention to her hair. It took nearly two hours, but it finally happened. Amelia changed the shade of her hair. It wasn't much, and it wasn't the color she had hoped for, but it was certainly much lighter than it had been.

"Very good!" Margit said out loud. "Practice every day. Turn a red apple green. Change the color of your eyes. In fact, learn to shield the whites of your eyes so you can cast openly without causing fear. As you know, people aren't fond of us. Start with these small things and work hard at them. Meditation will give you the rest you need to continue."

Amelia felt excited. With Zoe coming along, she knew that she could continue lessons and possibly learn even more. The art of storytelling the way the mystics did it was nothing short of amazing.

Master storytellers like Zoe would tell or listen to the story of another and project images for everyone else to see. The tale would play out for them as if they had been there.

That was the same type of spell that might be needed in times of battle. With that kind of power, one could make an enemy believe they were surrounded by men, or snakes, or spiders— anything the mystical magic user might have need for at that time.

Additionally, Margit helped Amelia learn how to strengthen her own barriers, a lesson Arryn had also been working on with Zoe since the thoughts of the others in the room had come flooding in.

Even if Amelia wasn't able to use mental abilities to change their position in the battle to come, she was very confident those mystics would have one hell of a time getting into their heads.

CHAPTER SIXTEEN

S carlett once again stood on the Capitol steps as she faced her people, pushing as much charm as she could on those in front so it would spread. Nikolai and Barbara stood behind her to help with the effort.

Unbeknownst to the crowd, there were several other mystics now wandering among them, affecting emotions and creating a sense of comfort and intense loyalty in Scarlett's presence.

This would not fail.

Scarlett wanted to test her hold on her people, and she knew exactly how to do it. Her newly-arrived friends would pick out the weakest among them—more than likely Boulevard scum— and use them to incite a riot, one that her extremely *loyal* people would have to take care of in her honor.

If nothing else, it would be very amusing—to her.

"With everything that has happened lately, I felt that I should address you face to face. You have suffered so much. The remnant invasion. The betrayal of your former Chancellor. The death of Talia. The loss of so many members of our trusted and brave Guard. And now…"

She lowered her head, shaking it a little as her brows creased.

CANDY CRUM & MICHAEL ANDERLE

She could feel her friends mentally pushing against the crowd, making them feel terrible for her as they watched her performance.

Scarlett momentarily placed her hand to her mouth just before wiping at nonexistent tears. It looked real enough to the crowd.

"And now, we have suffered another loss. Several more guards were killed, including two of my closest friends, people who were helping me find ways to better protect the city. But no... Arryn didn't want that. *Amelia* didn't want that. They came in the night, just as they did before, and they took them from us."

The crowd began to get worked up as her words carried not only her influence, but that of the mystics in the crowd. A handful of those people began to feel rage. A sense of duty, but not to her.

To Amelia. To Arryn.

These people, who were no different than any other innocent man or woman in the crowd, were being overwhelmed by Scarlett's new friends. Scarlett only needed to continue exactly as she was for this to work.

"How many times will we let them do this? How many times will we allow them to sneak in here and take the lives of those closest to us? When is enough enough?" Scarlett shouted.

The crowd responded even more enthusiastically, shouting their appreciation and support for her.

"Amelia is working with her. With Arryn. They *won't* stop—not until they have what they want! We had no idea what that was, but now I fear they desire the death of every man, woman, and child in this city."

She paused for a moment to allow that to sink in. As she looked at the crowd, she saw a few people moving forward, their faces creased with anger.

Keep pushing, Scarlett, Kade, one of the mystics in the crowd, told her. *Keep talking. It's all about to crash.*

"Amelia is a traitor to this city, and we *must* stop her! She and Arryn have declared war on us time and time again. *Who is with me?* Who will stand with me and fight for Arcadia? Who will help me kill our enemies so our children might live?"

As the shouts began and their fists went into the air, declaring both their excitement and their devotion to her cause, a fight broke out—and then another.

Scarlett jumped, her hands moving to cover her mouth in feigned shock as she watched with utter joy. The plan was working perfectly.

"Fuck you!" one of the men shouted as guards seized him. "Those men deserved to die!"

Scarlett's brows creased as a disgusted expression replaced the one of abject horror she had worn only a moment before. "Why? How can you say that? These men and women were our Arcadian brothers and sisters! They were innocent!"

The man pulled hard against the men holding him, ready to charge at Scarlett the moment he got the opportunity.

"There are more of us than you! You won't stop us! We will stop at *nothing* to take back the city!" he shouted.

"For Amelia!" another man shouted as he pulled a knife from his belt and jammed it into the throat of guard standing next to him.

The crowd went wild as the mystics sent the men they controlled into a frenzy, attacking guards and screaming various things in support of Amelia and Arryn.

Soon, the Guard had them on the ground in magitech cuffs, though a few had lost their lives.

Scarlett hadn't expected quite that level of a show, but it really had been perfect. Even better than she had expected, and it was *exactly* what she needed.

She raised her hands in the air as the "traitors" were carried away. "Everyone! Please!"

Scarlett waited for a few moments, giving the shaken crowd

time to calm. The tension could have been cut with a knife. Their neighbors knew the men who had attacked as gentle souls who had always worked for the city and helped their fellow man.

That was exactly who they *had* been—until her talented friends had gotten hold of them.

"This has to stop. We have tried to allow the city to move on naturally, but that isn't working. We're allowing them to control us. I say *enough!* Now is the time to take back control of *our* city, and end this war for good. Go with me to the Dark Forest, and I *promise* you... We will take Arcadia back!"

The crowd screamed and cheered, determination on their faces.

They are yours, Kade sent telepathically. *Tell us what you want, and we will do it. We need to plan for the Dark Forest.*

Scarlett turned, smiling as she began to walk back inside the Capitol building. *Have them gather the materials. I will have the Guard prepare.*

As ELYSIA, Rae, and Alehah rode into the Dark Forest, Elysia began to worry about telling her father what had happened. He had been worried about her; hadn't thought it wise for her to ride to Arcadia.

It wasn't that he had been right. She'd had the best of intentions, and things had been going well. They'd had everything they needed. The information wasn't as detailed as she would have liked, but they'd had enough to craft a well-thought-out plan for Arryn's and Cathillian's attack.

Now that was ruined. Now two of the five mystics were dead, and there was no way to predict what Scarlett was going to do about it. Would she bother to replace them at all? Would she only replace the two she had lost? Or would she get pissed off and import an army of mystics?

Elysia sure as hell knew what *she* would have done in that situation.

The entire trip had been pointless. Everything they had learned had been negated by Alehah and her need to test her skills. What was worse, Elysia had allowed the girl to manipulate her.

The Elder had known better than to let that happen. She had known the girl was wrong, but when she began talking about the risk to Cat and Arryn... Well, Elysia couldn't stand by and allow that to happen. The girl had played on her motherly instincts, knowing she would get what she wanted.

Alehah had fought in minor skirmishes before, and had even fought the dark druids when they came for Jenna and her parents. She was no stranger to battle. What she hadn't been able to do, however, was test her strengths as an assassin. Then again, not many *Schatten* had.

The shadow warriors grew up training hard. They knew how good they were, and they were tested among their own. There were times when they were needed, but most times they were only there to strategically affect the outcome of war.

Alehah had dramatically overstepped her bounds, and their people would pay for it. Without a doubt in her mind, Elysia knew it was impossible for the Arcadians to sit quietly now.

They would more than likely believe it had been Arryn, and potentially Amelia as well. There was no reason for them to think it had been Elysia, because they had never seen her—or any other druid besides Cathillian, for that matter.

As a result, they would come for Arryn in the only other place they would know to find her.

The Dark Forest.

How could she tell her father she had made a mistake? That she had allowed herself to lose focus and be discovered? If they had finished and left before Alehah had started in, they would have gotten off scot-free.

No one would have known they had been there, and war would not have come for them quicker. Deep down, Elysia wondered if they could survive a war with the Arcadians without Arryn's help. Without Amelia.

They entered the southern village, and Elysia's father approached them with a smile. His arms were outstretched as he welcomed her.

"Daughter! I'm so glad you're home. All three of you safe and sound! The governor, his son Nathaniel, and those we sent with them have all returned safely as well." He made his way to her, hugging her as she dismounted Chaos. "How did your journey go?"

She pulled away, her eyes finding his and just staring at him. She opened her mouth a few times to speak, but couldn't find the words to say.

"I…" she began, but stopped.

The Chieftain's brows furrowed as he studied his daughter. "What is it?"

She opened her mouth again, but another voice spoke.

"Chieftain," Alehah said. "I believe it's me you should speak with regarding this."

Elysia turned, her eyes wide as the girl stood there, shoulders square, feet shoulder-width apart, and hands clasped behind her back.

"Oh?" the Chieftain said. "What happened? What is this about?"

Alehah cleared her throat. "Everything went great. We got in without being seen, and we got all the information we needed."

The Chieftain nodded. "This sounds good so far."

Alehah nodded. "It was, sir. But… But then I got carried away."

His eyes narrowed. "How do you mean?"

"I've lived here my entire life. I've never left. When I saw the chance to fully test my training… I don't know, I just *needed* to.

Before you say anything, no. That is no excuse, but it *is* the reason."

Elysia wanted to interject. It should have been her giving her father the rundown of what had happened, but she couldn't deny her curiosity regarding what Alehah would say. Not only that, but she wanted to judge her father's reaction before he said anything.

"Continue," the Chieftain ordered.

"We learned there were five mystics in the city. While there weren't enough to give them a fully controlled army, there were certainly enough to turn the general populace against Arryn and Amelia and set them against the Dark Forest. I thought…" She sighed. "I thought if we could just thin them out, we would stand a chance. I thought about Arryn and Cathillian getting hurt, when all we had to do was take one or two out and weaken their defenses. It's what we train for!"

"Elysia," the Chieftain turned to his daughter. "You supported this?"

"Absolutely not," Rae chimed in before Elysia could speak. "Like me, Elysia was against it. She was worried for her son and goddaughter, but she knew engaging would have been a terrible idea. Unfortunately, as it was being discussed, we were overheard."

The Chieftain gave an annoyed laugh. "The *Schatten* were overheard? Really?"

Rae nodded as she swallowed. "Yes, sir."

Alehah spoke up. "A mystic felt us there. One overpowered me and forced me to attack Elysia. You should know that if it hadn't been for her, I would have died there. She knocked me out and got me over the wall to safety. After that, I don't know what happened."

Rae nodded. "After that, we fought the guards who had been alerted. I'm not entirely sure if they heard us or if they were alerted by the mystics, but regardless, we fought them and won. We killed two mystics and fled."

The Chieftain turned to Elysia. "Is this what happened?"

She swallowed. It was mostly true. Both women were covering for her weakness. Elysia was a woman of honor, and the idea of lying to her father didn't sit well with her. However, knowing that he would look at her with pity made her feel even more unsettled.

"Yes," Elysia said again, once again feeling like a sixteen-year-old girl.

The Chieftain sighed before turning to Alehah. "I'm sorry, but you senselessly risked not only your own life, but those of two others, one of them your Elder. I have no choice but to relieve you of your position. The *Schatten* warriors are a very elite and important part of our army. You have proven you can't handle the responsibility."

Silent tears slid down Alehah's face as she nodded, doing her best to hold her head just as high as she had earlier. "Yes, sir. Does this mean that I am no longer a warrior? If so, I humbly request to be allowed to train others. I might not be fit to fight alongside everyone, but I still have the skills necessary to teach."

The Chieftain thought for a few moments. "You will be limited to patrol and training duties. We will see where you go from there." He turned to Elysia. "Do you have anything to add?"

Elysia's eyes lingered on her father's for a few seconds before turning them to Alehah. The girl gave a brief smile and nodded.

Elysia shook her head. "No. I think this punishment is fitting. She can join me on patrol and in training duties for her first week."

"Thank you, Elysia," Alehah said.

"We might not have a week," the Chieftain reminded her.

All attention turned to him, and there was silence before Elysia finally nodded.

"Unfortunately, this news brings great consequences," the Chieftain said.

"I've thought about that," Elysia replied.

He placed his hand on his daughter's shoulder. "Good, because we have to ready everyone. We will also need to make use of the Cellan Guard. War is coming, daughter, and I fear it will be upon us very soon."

CHAPTER SEVENTEEN

A laric and his people arrived in the Terres Forest early in the morning, the birds chirping in the trees as they walked the paths. He had given strict instructions that no one was to attempt using magic once they had entered, including taming anything. It was hard to say how his brother would take such behavior.

Unlike Alaric, Jerick and his people walked a thin line between the peace and structure that Alexander of the Dark Forest had set for his people and the culture of total freedom Alaric had set for his.

The Terres druids did as they pleased, but they were taught respect. It was the only law of Jerick's land. Respect one another —but anything else is yours to take.

Living this way allowed his druids to retain their healthy nature magic, but also harness the power that Alaric had, though it had been scaled down. They were able to grow healthy fruit and keep their forest lush, though it would never compare to the Dark Forest.

As they walked along they saw bears, leopards, and birds of various species, all healthy. All cloaked in beautiful fur or feathers. All of them stunning. It had been many years since Alaric had come to see his brother, and he now remembered why he hadn't.

Because he hated what he had built.

Even had Alaric known what would happen, he would do it all again—and that was exactly what he planned to do. That was the true reason why he wanted the Dark Forest. He wanted to give his people a fair shot, so they could live like his brother.

If Jerick wanted a cantaloupe, he grew one. If he wanted coin, he would steal it or kill for it. But if a man, woman, or child sheltered under the canopy of his trees, no harm would come to them—because that would be considered dishonorable. They were family.

Alaric planned to test just how far that family loyalty went.

Unlike in the Dark Forest, there was no wall here to barricade Jerick from the outside world. Instead, anyone was able to approach, but if he judged against whoever dared to enter, he would destroy them before they could even defend themselves.

Alaric could see the small wooden homes from a distance. Unlike the living-tree homes in the Dark Forest, these were small structures crafted from wood that had been harvested from the forest around them. These druids had no issue cutting down trees. It made a lot more sense than bending and shaping trees into a house.

Before they made it the rest of the way to the village, something fell from a tree just ahead of them. Vines burst from the ground and grasped what appeared to be a small girl before lowering her to the ground.

She had very kinky and thick, dark-grey hair, its color not much different than Alaric's. It was disheveled and matted, with leaves and sticks tangled in it. Her dark-grey skin was covered in filth. When her eyes snapped open, he saw they glowed a very bright green—almost a neon green.

He had only seen that color in one other druid's eyes— Alexander's.

Alaric couldn't help but think just how cute she would have been had she not been filthy and worn tattered clothing. She was seven or eight at most, so he wondered where her parents were.

As far as Alaric knew, Jerick's people didn't live in filth. They were at least moderately clean, though not everyone bathed in the river regularly.

"Hello," Alaric said. "Do you know who I am?"

Her eyes flashed brighter as Alaric took a step closer. She growled at him—actually *growled*. The girl bared her crooked teeth at Alaric as she lowered herself into a defensive position.

"He don't want you," was all she said.

Alaric smiled. "So, you *do* know who I am."

"Ya look just like 'im, but bad. You're a bad man," she said.

His eyes narrowed. Jerick didn't judge others' behavior, and he sure as hell didn't teach his people to do so either. The only thing the Terres druids cared about was if someone planned to hurt or steal from them. If either of those were possibilities, they had a problem. Past that, it didn't matter who you loved, hated, fucked, or killed, as long as they didn't reside in his forest.

So, why would the little girl think Alaric was a bad man?

"I don't think you know me at all, little one. Where are your parents?" Alaric asked.

"They're bad, too. You're all bad." She spat on the ground, achieving an impressive distance to almost hit Alaric's bare feet.

He smiled again. "Interesting. I think I see now why you're a filthy little beast. You believe you're better than everyone. Is that it? Mommy and Daddy teaching you the lesson that you're not?"

She shook her head. "Oh, I *know* I'm better than you."

In a flash, the girl disappeared into the trees, the vines having carried her away so quickly, he wondered how her neck didn't break.

"What a strange child," Aeris said from beside him.

Alaric nodded. "Strange indeed. Let's go." He nodded to where a man stood in a clearing. "My brother's waiting for us."

AFTER A SECOND NIGHT in the Heights, they made one hell of an early start the next morning. She and her companions had to get back. They wanted to make it back long before the dark druids, so they had a chance to prepare. If their enemies were lucky in their travels and managed to get help from the dark druids to the west, it was highly possible they wouldn't go south.

They would march east, straight into the Dark Forest.

In her short amount of time in the temple, Arryn had trained hard in a form of magic she not only didn't understand, but really didn't enjoy. Delving into the minds of others still seemed like an invasion of privacy to her, but she had been grateful for the lessons.

Now if she were to use too much energy after a big battle, she would be able to meditate to regain some strength. She still wasn't clear if it worked *during* a battle, if she were able to steal a few moments in safety, but she assumed that it probably wouldn't be a good idea anyway.

While meditation had been a great lesson to learn, the mental shields she had learned to put up had been the best lesson of all. If she or anyone else were to stand a chance against Scarlett and her friends, those would be a necessity.

Everyone had come to stand just outside the Temple to see them off, and Arryn, Amelia, and Zoe turned to face Margit. She never looked quite *happy*, but that was just her. She was a very kind woman, albeit one with a take-no-shit attitude.

"Zoe, take care of yourself in your journeys. Julianne would hate me if anything happened to you," Margit said.

The younger mystic smiled. "I'll be fine, Margit. Like the battle with Adrien, this is our fight, too. They've taken Arcadia, and I think it's only a matter of time before they go for the Dark Forest. What do you think will happen once they've done that?"

Margit nodded. "Those were the very same reasons Julianne gave for her journey—the potential danger to us and the Temple."

"We will return her to you soon," Amelia said with a smile. "If there's anything I've learned, it's 'don't underestimate determined young women.' They thrive on challenges."

Margit eyed Amelia for a moment before turning her gaze to Zoe. "You have your work cut out for you, going against so many, but I do have faith in you."

The women saluted Margit before saying their goodbyes, and everyone else followed suit. She stood outside with Nigel and watched the group leave.

"I BARELY SAW you the whole time we were here," Arryn said to Cathillian as they started down the mountain. This time, she rode on Snow's back with Dante in tow as the others rode horses that had been loaned to them by the mystics.

He shrugged. "I was working with Nigel, actually. He showed me some pretty cool tricks. Why? Ya miss me?"

She scoffed, then laughed. "Not hardly, though I *did* miss Dante. His mother and I couldn't help but notice you had possession of him most of the time. You only brought him back when he was hungry."

"Well, I sure as hell didn't have the parts to feed him," Cathillian quipped.

Arryn shook her head. "Anyway, you said you learned some stuff? Really? I figured you'd be hardcore against it, being a native druid and all."

There was a pause as Cathillian's expression turned serious. "A few months ago, I would have said you were damn right about that one. But that was then, and this is now. I have people to protect—you most of all. I'm not going to pass up the opportunity to make my chances of doing that greater."

The way he looked at her then reminded her of the way he had looked at her in the pond. He had been so determined to tell her in his own way that he cared for her, and his expression had mirrored that. Now, it was very much the same.

Then she remembered the kiss, and she blushed and turned away.

Arryn only smiled and nodded, facing forward and silently asking Snow to move faster. She couldn't stand to be back there with him any longer.

They reached Craigston in very little time. The trip had been shortened by hours since the last one. They had been descending, which would have made it faster all on its own, but being able to use animals that were used to making that trip often hastened it even more.

When they reached Ophelia's to swap the Temple's horses for their own, Samuel was waiting for them. "It's about damn time! I been waitin' here all mornin'!"

"How did you even know we were coming?" Arryn asked. "I figured we'd have to get you from home."

"A shipment of brew went out this morning," Zoe said with a smile. "I might have passed the message along."

"Yeah. And those old bastards got here a lot quicker than any of ye, and they were carryin' barrels on their backs!" Samuel grumbled.

Arryn looked at him incredulously. "On their backs? You're full of shit, old man."

Samuel shook his head. "It's good ta see ye, too, lass. We ready ta go?"

"Yeah, and we better get going if we want to avoid the bandits on the road," Celine said as she walked up.

Arryn had sobered a little from the brew she had drunk that morning. It hadn't been much, and the brew didn't get people drunk—just good and tipsy so they could relax and allow their minds to rest. She had felt it would be a good idea to have a drink with Zoe and Margit before leaving.

Her mind wandered back to the trip to Craigston, the very night they had arrived in the small rearick town. They had come across a group of rearick who were under attack just north of the mountains.

She didn't find out until later that evening when they dropped them off at the small medical building in Craigston that it had been bandits. People had been attacking the rearick on their journeys and stealing crystals and brew.

She definitely wanted to avoid an altercation of any kind if possible. Though it had only been a few days, she felt like an entirely different person. She had been ready for an adventure then, but now the weight of the world was settling back in on her, and she wanted to be careful.

The group chatted casually as they traveled down the mountain, but by the time they reached the bottom and were able to break into a full gallop, everyone was silent. Arryn couldn't explain it, but something felt off. The feeling of dread had returned, and all she wanted was to get home to the Forest.

CHAPTER EIGHTEEN

Alaric had been surprised at the warm welcome his brother Jerick had given him. They had hugged one another, and Jerick had given him a tour through the village. Now, more than ever, Alaric wanted to live like that.

He wanted to wake up to the scent of life instead of decay. He wanted to taste real fruit.

When the dark druids grew plants, the plants matured with something very wrong with them. They would be half-dead, rotted. The fruits and vegetables always smelled terrible, but their bodies healed quickly, so they ate it.

Living in such a way, along with the effects of the dark magic itself, it gave them greyish skin and made some of them look much older than what they were, even though they were capable of living just as long as the druids of the Dark Forest.

The dark chieftain was through with this. He wanted his people to take a few steps back, to begin to come back into the light. It wouldn't happen without a fight, though—one he didn't plan to have until *after* he secured the Dark Forest.

If his people knew what he planned to do, they wouldn't help him. They were selfish assholes who would sell their own mothers if it got them something shiny. He despised each and every one of them, but they were his responsibility, and because of that, he cared.

That was why he enjoyed Aeris so much. Aeris, like Jerick, was able to walk the line between being respectful and practicing good magic while taking what he wanted when he wanted it. It was because of this that Aeris could continue to grow his own food, even after all that time.

His sister was a bit more volatile, though, and Alaric knew he would have to get control of her before she went too far off the deep end like the rest of his followers.

Alaric didn't care how his goal of taking over the druids' lands was achieved. He didn't care how many innocent men, women, children, and their filthy companions he had to rip apart. He *would* have the Dark Forest, and he *would* have his new beginning.

He hoped being in the Terres Forest would help his people see what life could be like if they only changed their ways a little.

"I'm happy to have you here, Brother," Jerick began, "though I was sorry to learn the reason for the trip."

"You don't have to pretend with me, Brother. We both know you want to say it," Alaric replied.

Jerick smiled. "I don't delight in your misfortune, though, yes —you're very right. I was pretending in order to spare you. We both know I warned you this would happen. Granted, I had no idea the extent to which it would go, but I knew something would happen."

Alaric examined his brother. They didn't look very different from one another. Jerick was dark-skinned and attractive, just as Alaric was. His hair was only a few shades lighter than Alaric's, but his eyes were green. Not because of his magic, though—they were the same color green their mother once had when she had been alive.

"How is it we are so alike, but so different?" Alaric asked.

Jerick shrugged. "It's always boiled down to respect. You were impatient. You wanted what you wanted, and you needed to have it right then. When Alexander put rules on you, instead of taking the time to adjust you cried 'injustice' and plotted against him."

Alaric shifted his stance, his arms crossing over his chest as his eyes narrowed. "You did the same, if I remember."

Jerick smiled. "Yes, I did. My brother was gone, and Alexander was stubborn. He was more concerned with rules and laws than the loss of one of our own. I wouldn't stand for that. When I left, I didn't agree with either one of you." He gestured around. "And that's how I ended up with this. Neutrality, brother."

Shaking his head, Alaric said, "Yes, well, neutrality got you this while your own brother wasted away in whatever cave he could find to call home before the druids of the Dark Forest came to run him off. You have no idea what it's like to hate someone as much as I hate Alexander. He took *everything* from me."

"You *know* the story is more complicated than that," Jerick replied, placing a hand on Alaric's tense shoulder. "I don't like him any more than you do, but *you* threw out what made us who we are. As you can see, you can still live free and not be weighed down by someone who thinks he knows better than everyone."

Alaric laughed. "Yeah, but that someone is me now."

Jerick smiled. "Pride is what gets you in trouble. When you left, you hated things so much that you did everything you could to undo the druid way of life. You succeeded, didn't you?"

He knew Jerick was talking about his people and just how opposite they were. In that respect, he had definitely been successful, but it had destroyed his followers.

"Enough about this," Jerick said. "I have a gift for you. A peace offering. After all this time, you've come back. When you leave, I want us to be brothers again. No more talk about the past. You came here because you want to take the Dark Forest, yes?"

Alaric hadn't had the chance yet to get to that, but his brother already knew. "Yes. I want all of this. I want to undo the damage I've done. For that, Alexander and his people must die."

Jerick smiled. "Very good. You know, once you claim that forest as your own, we'll be neighbors. *Nothing* will stop us then. We will have anything we want. No one will ever stand in our way again."

When he had decided to come to the Terres Forest, Alaric had had no idea what to expect from his brother. He had been unsure if he would be met with violence or indifference, but he certainly hadn't expected *this*.

It was everything he could have wished for and more.

"What is this gift? Because the future you just spoke of…" He smiled. "Let's make that happen. I thought I would get what I wanted with the Dark Forest, but with you by my side—family again—I truly *would* have everything."

Wrapping his arm around Alaric's shoulders, Jerick pulled him away from the village. "I know your people have a hard time growing plants, but this one is nearly impossible to kill. It grows with minimal water, and it will flourish with more. It has very potent fruit, but the leaves are incredibly powerful, too."

"Powerful how?" he asked.

"The tree isn't native to this area, but we have spent time cultivating it. When it rains, the tree oozes white sap that will burn anyone who touches it. We dip our arrows in the sap. Even when dry it's fatal, and the death is horribly painful. I will give you some seeds from the fruit, but don't eat the fruit."

Alaric smiled. "What about the leaves? You mentioned they were strong, too."

"This is the best part. If you were to burn the leaves and use the wind to push smoke into the Dark Forest, I can promise you won't have much of a fight on your hands."

Alaric's eyes widened as he stared at his brother, hope building. Before he could say a word, Jerick continued.

"We have a natural tolerance for the smoke because of our

tolerance for poisons due to our magic, but still, mishandling it will result in illness for some. You, however, have an advantage that even I don't have. Your bodies are used to processing poisonous food. You survive on it because it is most of what you can grow. These leaves will have no effect on you."

"And anyone else?" Alaric asked.

"The smoke will blind anyone who stands in its way. It will also cause severe breathing problems, and anyone who is older or very young will more than likely die. Everyone else will become so weak and ill that you can easily strike while they are down. Their bodies won't be able to heal from this fast enough, I can promise you that," Jerick explained.

There was a rustling in the trees above, momentarily catching their attention. They looked up, but saw nothing.

"I assume that was your little feral girl," Alaric said. "I met her earlier. She's quite a treat."

Jerick laughed. "Oh, yes. Her own parents don't even want her. She isn't like the rest of us. We celebrate differences, but that girl is wild. 'Feral' is a very appropriate description. She doesn't belong here. You're free to take her with you, if you think you can tame her."

Sharing in the laugh, Alaric shook his head and turned back to Jerick. "No, I think I'm good. She told me I'm terrible, and I'm pretty sure she'd rather die than have anything to do with me or my people anyway. As for the rest of this… Thank you. Not even Alexander will be able to stand in our way now."

Jerick shook his head. "No. In fact, with the seeds to these plants, no one will."

YOUNG CORRINE WATCHED from the trees as the strange man met with their chieftain. She could tell by looking they were related, but she hadn't ever seen him before.

That hadn't mattered to her. She could sense it all over him. He was a terrible man.

Curiosity had gotten the better of her, though, and she had decided to take to the trees to watch everything unfold. Living on her own, she was forced to fend for herself. Unlike anyone else here, the animals actually liked her.

They only tolerated the rest of the jerks in the village. She doubted the new man and his people were even tolerated. She could hear it in the way the birds chirped. They didn't like the men and women who had come through.

Corrine was only eight years old, but in that time she had become a very powerful nature magic user. The others practiced in case something bad ever happened, but she practiced to survive.

Without her magic, she would have died long ago. The other kids hated her and bullied her. They treated her terribly, and her parents hadn't done much to stop it. They were always off helping their chieftain with something.

She had nearly been killed by some terrible kids and their familiars. That day she had vowed never to let anyone take advantage of her or hurt her again.

Day in and day out, she practiced. Only three years had passed, but in that time she had grown exponentially—even if her size didn't reflect it.

She was nearly silent as she went through the trees. No one could hear her approach, even on the ground. That man had been wrong when he said it was her. Yes, she had been in the tree, but a few squirrels playing had startled a flock of birds that rustled the trees. Not her.

Still, she took that opportunity to do something she had wanted to do for a long time, but had had no idea how. She hadn't had the courage.

Until then.

Once her chieftain began to tell his brother what he had been growing, she knew where her parents had been and what they had been doing. They had been creating a plant that could cause a lot of people to get hurt—or worse.

Corrine wouldn't stand for that.

The people of the Dark Forest had to be warned. She was surrounded by bad people. People with no souls. Surely their enemy weren't worse than them. At least, she hoped that was the case.

Either way, it would get her away from the Terres Forest and take her on a journey. They wouldn't miss her. She was sure they wouldn't even know she was gone. That would give her time.

It had been a long time, but she had once traveled to the edge of their forest. It would take a couple of days to cut straight through, but she had to make it before they did. She had to save them if she could.

Corrine only hoped that she found people worth saving when she arrived.

CHAPTER NINETEEN

Scarlett rode behind row after row of guardsmen, as she herself followed the Arcadian magicians—some of those very men and women riding horses that pulled carts full of oil barrels behind them. They were the ones who would help her realize her plan.

Her friends were carefully stationed among the rows as they rode toward the Dark Forest, and she couldn't help but smile as she realized her struggle was about to be over. Everything was going to fall into place.

She had been inside the southern village in the Dark Forest when the dark druids retrieved Jenna. Although she didn't know much about the Chieftain, his family, or any of the other druids who resided there, she had to assume it was too far from the edge of their villages within their barrier for them to sense anything the Arcadians were about to do.

What are your orders? Lacy asked.

She was Nikolai's sister, and had so far proven to be very useful. She was working with Kade in the mass of guardsmen, gently pushing feelings of motivation and determination.

We are getting close, Scarlett answered. *In another mile, the Guard will stop, and we will send the magicians forward.*

So far, the entire unit had moved as smoothly as any magitech machine she had ever seen. Each piece working in sync with the others. Each part serving a purpose. Given how atrociously trained the recently increased Guard had been when she came to Arcadia, she couldn't believe just how far they had come.

Arryn and Amelia had no idea who they were fucking with.

As they approached the place they would halt, Scarlett could hear shouts ahead. The Guard had stopped and left aisles wide enough for the magicians to pass through with the carts full of oil.

"Magicians!" Scarlett shouted to the magic users behind her, as well as with those pulling the carts behind their horses. "Move forward!"

Scarlett bit her lip to keep herself from smiling as she watched them execute the movements they had practiced just outside the Arcadian walls. For two days she had drilled them on the plan, and the squad leaders had tested them to make sure they remembered their parts without fail. If something happened, or if the druids sensed their arrival, the magicians couldn't be risked.

Those whose horses pulled carts went first, and the magicians followed closely behind as they made their way through the gaps in the Guard formation.

Scarlett was in charge of the magicians and walked down the center aisle until she reached the front line. "Front lines! Fan out!"

She turned her head from side to side as she watched the Guard's front two lines fan out in a semi-circle, which left the magicians exposed, but in a position where they could quickly cover them.

"Magicians, *go!*" Scarlett called out.

Rows of eyes flashed black as the magicians began to call their magic. Several guards punctured large holes in the tops of the barrels as pairs of magic users went to work. One would levitate the barrel as the other manipulated the liquid inside it.

Some of the oil would be sprayed above the canopy while other magicians tried to reach the vegetation underneath. Given how close they were to the forest and the number of barrels of oil they had brought along, they would be able to coat a large portion before they set it on fire.

We have scouts watching for Arryn, Kade sent. *Try to relax. Everything is going well.*

He was right, but watching everything move so smoothly was giving her anxiety. As the barrels were lifted from their carts, the magicians carefully levitating them over the trees, her apprehension became even worse.

We have to hurry, Scarlett sent to the mystics in her employ.

The wind picked up as the oil spilled, and a cold chill ran down Scarlett's spine.

Can anyone sense anything? she sent. *The wind could be the druids.*

Scarlett, Nikolai sent, *it's just the wind. There are clouds in the sky, as there have been all day. This is natural.*

She shook her head, taking several deep breaths before exhaling. *That doesn't matter. It won't be long. We* must *move faster.*

For the first time since she had arrived in Arcadia, she felt a moment of panic. Normally, she was very calm and collected. Nothing bothered her—unless it was a hitch in a plan.

The barrels are empty, Lacy sent.

Scarlett nodded, though she knew the mystic couldn't see the response. "Light the bitch up," she said to the magician standing only a few feet in front of her, her voice sounding far more confident than she felt.

There was a flicker of something in the magician's face. Hesitation. Looking into the woman's mind, Scarlett saw that she was questioning her leadership. She wondered if this was the way things should be done.

Scarlett pushed against her, filling her mind with a sense of loyalty and pride in their cause. Finally, the woman smiled, turned, and arced her hands over her chest.

One by one, the other magicians followed suit as they created large fireballs.

"Loose!" Nikolai shouted.

The rain of fire ripped through the sky, and the forest exploded into flames. But they didn't stop. They threw more fireballs into places where the oil hadn't been poured, orange and red immediately flicking to life in the brush on the ground.

Within only a couple of minutes, thick black smoke filled the sky as the Forest was consumed. Birds everywhere took to the sky, blacking out what little was left of the sun before they scattered to the north.

As Scarlett realized what was happening and remembered the one piece of the puzzle she had forgotten, it was too late. The birds were airborne, flying to safety. Flying for *help*.

We need to move now! Scarlett sent to every mystic in the crowd. Panicking, she turned her horse and began to run back through the gaps in formation, others taking note as she did.

But before she could get far, a deep, earth-shaking clap of thunder boomed overhead, stopping her and everyone else in their tracks as fear grabbed them.

More chills seized Scarlett as the rolls of thunder slowly dwindled. Her eyes widened, and she turned her head to look for what she had heard in the midst of the rumbles—a growl so loud that she had at first thought it was more thunder.

She had heard it before. It was the sound of a bear.

Her eyes darted upward when she heard a loud screech pierce the skies. She saw a bird that she had seen before—in the mind of Talia, when she had met Cathillian.

"Fuck," she said out loud.

What is it? Nikolai asked.

Scarlett looked around, searching for any face that was truly loyal to her, but they were surrounded by the sheep.

We're surrounded.

"What do you mean, 'surrounded?'" Barbara asked as she came up to Scarlett and Nikolai from behind.

Scarlett looked up once again and saw that Echo had turned and was now flying back south.

"Arryn's coming."

THE CHIEFTAIN HAD BEEN busy with the children, training them how to heal wounded plants, when the first warning came. He and Elysia had known an attack was likely, so the perimeter had been extended to the eastern edge of the Dark Forest—not just the edge of their barrier.

Schatten posted high in the trees saw the army approaching from a couple of miles out and had sent birds to warn them. Luckily for them, they had also seen the barrels, and so had known the plan from the start.

They retreated, allowing the network of trees and their knowledge of their inner workings of the Forest to benefit them as they soared through the branches. Using vines, they moved as fast as any horse could have carried them. Even faster, for some.

The warriors had been placed on alert, and the Chieftain sent them out the moment the birds arrived with the messages. The druids began sending familiars out all over, warning the animals of the Dark Forest of what was to come.

Some fled, while other larger animals headed southeast, even with the threat of fire.

"Ride fast," the Chieftain told Elysia. "Don't wait for Zobig and me. I have plans."

With nothing more than a nod, Elysia jumped on Chaos' back. He had already knelt for her to mount. The Shire horse and his master ran hard then, more druids trailing them on their own horses.

The designated healers took to the trees with the *Shatten,* and the shadow warriors propelled them through as quickly as possible. The healers had no other responsibility—just as they did in training. They would keep the fighters from having to mend themselves.

The Chieftain watched his people effortlessly fall into their roles—the roles they trained for day in and day out—and checked around his village to make sure those who remained were safe as well.

Maddie helped the elderly to gather up the children and move toward the Kalt. There they would shield themselves in a barrier so tight and so thick that nothing could get through, the proximity of water ensuring it couldn't be burned.

"Zobig!" the Chieftain shouted.

The black bear roared as he approached, kneeling for the Chieftain to mount just as Chaos had for Elysia. The Chieftain climbed on, and the two ran into battle. A normal black bear could run as fast as a horse in short distances, and Zobig was both larger and stronger. He could nearly match Chaos in speed and endurance.

They ran for nearly a mile before the sky was blackened by the terrified birds flying wildly overhead. A few minutes after that, the smell of smoke hit him. It was thick and heavy, not the natural smell that wood gave off when it was burned. This carried something else. *Oil.*

"They will pay for this with their lives," he seethed, rage taking him over as terrified and injured animals fled through the trees.

His pure hatred erupted and his eyes flashed, the sky growing dark as a loud clap of thunder shook everything it touched.

ARRYN and her group saw the smoke as they rode through the Valley. Their pace had been leisurely until they saw the plumes rising above their home. Then the group saw the clouds over the Forest turn dark as the thunder ripped through the sky.

"That's the Chieftain!" Arryn called out. "Snow!"

Snow needed only to hear her name and she began to run at full speed toward the forest. Cathillian and the others followed as closely behind as they could manage.

"Echo!" Cathillian called out. "Find out what's happening."

The bird immediately changed direction, heading northwest toward the Forest.

"It's the Arcadians," Amelia said. "I just know it. They're making their move."

"I thought we would have more time!" Arryn shouted.

Within ten minutes, Echo returned, sending Cathillian the images of what she had seen.

"There's a whole fucking army," Cathillian reported.

Arryn didn't need to see Echo's images to know that. Her entire body radiated with anger as she realized exactly what this meant. Scarlett had made good on her promise.

Though she had threatened to burn the Forest several times, Arryn had never believed she would actually be brave enough—or stupid enough—to do it. Unfortunately for everyone involved, this battle would not be simple.

Not only did they have to save the Dark Forest, they had to find a way to fight without killing.

"Guys!" Arryn shouted toward her companions over their loud hoofbeats. "I know this will be hard, but you have to remember that these men and women are innocent."

"They're being controlled by the mystics," Amelia called back for anyone who could hear her. "Find a way to subdue rather than kill, if possible."

"But kill if necessary," Cathillian said.

When Arryn risked a look at him, she saw his brows creased

in deep concentration. She could actually feel the anger radiating off him, just as it was from her.

"It'll be okay," she said to him. "I took Talia's head for much less. Trust me, Cathillian. Believe me when I say that I will rip that bitch limb from limb. She will pay for every life lost on the battlefield."

He looked at her then, his eyes blazing green with the intense emotion he felt. His lips were pursed tight, and she could actually see how fearsome he would appear to anyone who crossed his path.

"Don't stop until you do," was all he said as he turned back and urged Maia to run even faster.

CHAPTER TWENTY

E lysia's heart felt as though it would stop as she rode up on the devastation before her. She could smell the oil that clung to the trees. It hadn't even been the darkness of a bad person that had caused this. This was pure evil, something cold and irrevocably broken. Something that could never be fixed.

In all her days, Elysia had never faced a foe capable of such a horrifying act. Burning the home of innocent life—man, woman, child, and animal alike.

Chaos huffed, his large front hooves repeatedly digging into the ground as if he itched to run into battle.

As she investigated the area, it became clear that the fire had been much hotter than normal, and in some places, it even burned blue. It had been magical fire—of that she was certain. The trees had already died and were charred so badly that going past them would mean risking the lives of everyone stalled behind her.

"Elysia," Ryel said. "We would follow you into hell. You need only lead us."

Tears threatened to fill her eyes as she prayed to the goddess that she would be worthy of such loyalty.

"The earth is dead here," she said. "We will be at the mercy of our opponents. Nothing will grow here until the fires are gone."

Thunder cracked again as the wind picked up, carefully blowing to the east away from the rest of the healthy trees. Rain began to fall, slowly at first. Elysia's eyes flashed as she lent her own power to her father's, bringing the rain down in sheets now.

"Elysia!" the Chieftain shouted as he rode up. "What are you doing?"

"The trees are gone. There is no life here. If we ride past them, I can't guarantee they won't collapse," she responded.

As the rain continued to pour, soaking them and their animals, the Chieftain smiled. "It will live again—but only if we do."

Screams echoed outside the forest loudly enough for them to hear, and a terrifying roar was quickly followed by a loud screech from the smoky sky.

The Chieftain laughed, the sound terrifying even Elysia. "Those Arcadians are *fucked* now."

It was Elysia's turn to smile. She turned back to Ryel. "Into hell it is!"

Chaos broke into a gallop, and Zobig was close behind as they headed toward the flames.

THE SCENE before them was nothing shy of heartbreaking. The smoke had gotten thicker and though rain now poured from the sky, it did nothing to quench the blaze wreaking havoc on the lush Forest she had called home for the majority of her life.

Arryn watched the Arcadians as they began to run back to their horses.

"They're trying to flee!" Arryn shouted.

Snow roared, alerting the army to her presence. At first, Arryn hadn't wanted her to do so, but when she heard their screams of terror and saw how disorganized they became, it warmed her.

"I've got this," Cathillian said, bloodlust tainting his voice.

His eyes glowed as he looked at the dark sky that had already darkened from his grandfather's magic. He lifted his hand, power emanating from him as bolts of lightning crashed into the path of the Arcadians, preventing them from going any farther.

"They *have* to know hell is coming for them," Celine shouted.

"They fucking will soon if they don't now!" Arryn bellowed.

"Remember," Amelia yelled, "save who you can!"

As a wall of guards began running toward Arryn and her group, she smiled. "Brute force. Got it."

"Give Dante to me," Celine called as she rode closer to Arryn.

Arryn lifted and hugged him, kissing him on the head, and Celine's eyes flashed black. She levitated the cub out of Arryn's hands and into hers. Without another word, Celine broke off and headed toward the stretch of Forest south of the fires. She would hide him and come back.

Once her baby was out of harm's way, Snow picked up the pace and ran headlong into battle. The tiger leapt into the air, clearing the heads of several guards before landing on several more. She dropped hard to the ground, crushing their legs as Arryn jumped free of her back.

"Good girl, Snow. Only kill if you have to," Arryn said, turning in time to throw an elbow into a guard's face.

Blood spurted from his nose as she kicked his knee hard enough to fold it backward. As he fell to his good knee, she brought her fist down on his temple, knocking him unconscious.

She pulled the staff from her back, knowing she would be most successful at preserving life using that weapon. A guard ran toward her, and she recognized him. Lionel. He was one of the students she had taught every morning with Cathillian.

"Lionel!" she called as he attacked. "You have to stop! We aren't your enemy, and you know it."

"You killed Talia," he shouted back as he threw an angry punch. He missed, clearly not remembering the lessons she had given him. "You killed all those guards. You're no friend of mine!"

He lunged again, and she countered with a right hook. Lionel leaned back in time for her to miss him, which caused her to spin slightly in the mud beneath her. Taking advantage of her bobble, he grabbed her around the waist and pulled her tightly against him.

As he went for her throat, she threw all her weight back, taking him down. After they landed, she threw the back of her head into his face, then turned over and straddled him.

"Remember! Talia was a psycho who ran me out of town. *She* killed all those kids, not me. Scarlett helped her. Scarlett is a mystic. Fight this, dammit!"

He groaned as he searched her face. His eyes slowly reflected understanding, followed quickly by guilt.

"No," Arryn snapped, "you don't have to feel guilty—not for something that wasn't your fault. Just get your ass up and help me get your brothers back."

Lionel nodded, wiping blood and mud from his face. Arryn stood, but was quickly thrown back to the ground. Her attacker still stood, but he was coming for her.

He brought his sword down, but she rolled out of the way before getting to her knees and grabbing his arm. She dropped, yanking him hard as she threw him over her back.

His sword fell from his hands, and she grabbed it, smashing him in the face with the hilt before he could seize her.

"Holy shit," Lionel said as he rushed over. "Why didn't you just kill him?"

She sighed, the corner of her mouth turning up in a sad smile. "Because I'm not the enemy. I'm here to save as many people as possible. I want you to do that, too. Break their legs. Their arms. Knock them out. Do whatever you have to take them down without killing them. We can heal *damage*. We *can't* heal death."

His brows furrowed as he stared at her. He swallowed then, nodding as he helped her up.

"Stop standing around before you die," Arryn said, clapping him on the shoulder before running back into the battle.

As ELYSIA RACED through the forest, she saw several Arcadians who had made their way across the threshold and were attacking the forest from the inside. Magicians were throwing fireballs, or simply spreading the fires that were already there.

Chaos ran forward, rearing onto his hind legs as Elysia slid off his back. As Chaos came back down, he kicked two Arcadian magicians in the chest, crushing their ribs and sending them to the ground panting for air.

Pulling the bow from her back, Elysia nocked her first arrow and loosed it, hitting a man in the leg before moving onto the next.

"What are you doing?" Ryel asked. "Quit maiming them. *Kill* them!"

The Chieftain and Zobig ran up, the black bear slamming into two men and pinning their legs with his front feet as his master attacked with his staff. "Save any that you can, Ryel. This is the work of a dark mystic. These men are innocent."

Ryel groaned as he went to work, cutting men down while trying to not to inflict life-threatening injuries.

A deep whine sounded, and the forest floor began to quiver beneath their feet. Along with the intense crackling of the fire, Elysia could hear one of the larger trees behind them beginning to give way.

"We have to get out of here!" Elysia called to the others. "The trees are starting to buckle."

The Chieftain looked up after taking another man down, having cracked him in the head with the butt of his staff. "The rain isn't touching the fire. The oil will have to burn off, or we will need physical magic users to stop the flames."

Elysia was about to respond when loud, determined cheers approached from just beyond the tree line. Turning, Elysia saw the governor and his men come running in, armed with staffs instead of swords—though they had those lashed to their belts.

"We have to take the fight to them," Elysia said. "They're trying to flee."

"Daughter," the Chieftain said. "We have to face the possibility that we might need to let them. This fire is magical. It's not going burn out anytime soon. If they get far enough away, the flames will die, but the longer they stay the longer these fires burn. You know as well as I do that we face losing much more than we have already."

"Move! Now!" Ryel shouted as the crackling tree began to crumble even faster, coming down before their very eyes.

Within seconds, the Chieftain was back on Zobig, and he pulled Elysia up with him as they charged out of the flames and onto the open battlefield. Elysia called for Chaos, making sure he got out safely as well.

As the black bear leapt the flames at the edge of the forest, Elysia's eyes were opened to just how big a conspiracy this had been. It didn't look like the entire Arcadian force was there, but there were no less than a third of them. If she were a betting woman, she would think maybe close to half. They had been fully prepared, and had come knowing exactly what to do.

She had no doubt that was Scarlett's doing.

Looking around, she saw several of their men on the ground, druid warriors who had lost their lives fighting Arcadians while fearing the loss of their home. As she and the Chieftain began to take in the horror they saw before them, Elysia saw Arryn fighting.

"Too many lives have been lost," the Chieftain said. "Arryn has turned some of the Arcadians back to her side, but it won't be enough. We have to stop the fire before it claims the entire forest."

Elysia didn't want that. She didn't want to let them go, but she knew he was right. The druid warriors were more than capable of fighting the Arcadians and winning, but not while the fear of losing the forest—their home, their source of food, and the habitat of so many animals—was at the front of their minds.

"Pull back!" the Chieftain shouted.

He stepped forward, throwing his hands out as he did. His eyes flashed neon-green and the grass grew wildly, wrapping around all the druids he could see and pulling them free of the battle. Elysia swallowed as she looked at Arryn.

The young woman's gaze was focused and her posture set. Elysia followed the direction in which her eyes were staring to find Scarlett, eyes white as she did her best to control her people.

Realization hit Elysia. If Arryn went for Scarlett, it wouldn't end well. She had to stop her. She had to save her.

WHEN IT HAD BECOME apparent that flight was no longer an option—bolts of lightning having struck the ground to keep them pinned—Scarlett had dismounted and headed into the battle, doing her best to control her people and keep them focused.

She only needed a little bit of magic for mind control. She was doing her best to save what was left for Arryn and the fight to come.

She had a feeling she would need it.

In the distance, she caught sight of a black bear, bigger than any she had ever seen. It exited the Forest with two druids on its back. That certainly wasn't good news, since she thought one of them might have been the Chieftain.

She turned to her left, trying to find Arryn. She needed to know where all her enemies were before she could continue.

CANDY CRUM & MICHAEL ANDERLE

Unfortunately for her, Arryn had been a bit more dangerous than she had given her credit for. The girl had known exactly how to fight in this unique situation and had been ready for anything and everything Scarlett threw at her.

Scarlett saw scattered bodies everywhere, but they weren't dead. Those men were alive, and they were looking at Arryn with admiration, even though they couldn't get up to fight any longer.

She had regained their trust, more than likely having knocked loose the mystics' control with severe trauma to the head, only to show her true colors by allowing them to live. Scarlett could see the images floating in the men's minds. She was a goddess to them, and they wanted nothing more than to fight by her side.

Others, those that she hadn't physically damaged but had managed to get through to mentally, fought by her side. They needed to leave soon, or Scarlett would lose everything.

Just as she was about to call for a retreat, Scarlett felt hatred burning into her from the other side of the battlefield. She looked across it; Arryn's eyes steadily locked on hers. A dark smile crossed the girl's face as she broke into a run.

Scarlett turned and raced back to her horse, mounting as grasses began whipping through the battlefield and snatching up the druids. It seemed as though the Chieftain was calling for a retreat as well, but she sure as hell wasn't going to stick around to find out.

She also wasn't about to challenge the most powerful druid in the world.

ARRYN HAD ALREADY TAKEN down more than a dozen men, and Cathillian was not far behind her. He had nearly matched her numbers, but he wasn't quite as fast since she had a staff to work with. So far, she had only had to kill two, and Cathillian had killed four. Given how many they had fought, she couldn't complain about the result.

She wouldn't allow them to have died in vain, though. She wouldn't allow *anyone* on that field to have died in vain.

When her eyes found the prize, she had been waiting to claim, she couldn't help the immense feeling of satisfaction that rose in her chest. She ran through a play-by-play of what she would do to Scarlett in her mind.

But fantasy just couldn't cut it. She wanted the real thing.

As she ran toward the mystic, she could hear Elysia calling to her over the sounds of violence. The druid called her name over and over, but Arryn wouldn't take her mind away from what she wanted most.

Something snaked around her waist, stopping her mid-run and yanking her back. When she landed, she was face to face with Elysia. "What the hell are you doing? I had her. I had Scarlett!"

Elysia only nodded. "I know, and I also know what I'm about to say won't make sense, but she's the least of our concerns right now. If the forest burns to the ground—and it is well on its way now—we'll lose everything. We'll have *nothing* to save."

Shaking her head, Arryn insisted, "No! I have to get her. I have to stop her!"

"Arryn! Stop. Please look around you. The Forest is in flames. Our brothers and sisters are dying out there, because all they can focus on is losing their home. We have to stop the fires. My father and I have tried, but we need a physical-magic user to make that happen."

Arryn turned and stared at the damage that had been dealt to the Forest. The fires had grown taller since she had gotten there. It was unreal to see so much of the forest gone in such a short time, despite the drenching rain.

Arryn searched for Scarlett, but she was completely out of sight now, and most of the men who had come with her had retreated. The physical magic users who were still alive had left with Scarlett as well. The rest were dead on the ground or incapacitated.

With Scarlett gone, the battle was beginning to wind down. There was no point in chasing her. First, they would save the Forest, and then...

Then she planned to make good on that promise she had made to Cathillian.

She planned to rip Scarlett limb from limb.

CHAPTER TWENTY-ONE

A rryn hadn't felt anything so gut-wrenching since—well, since watching Scarlett force hundreds of people to doing something they wouldn't normally do, effectively destroy her home.

Letting Scarlett just *walk away* had ripped her apart, but Elysia had been right. That bitch's time was coming—*soon.* Arryn had another job to do right then.

After she had walked into the blazing Dark Forest, she realized Elysia had made the right call. The areas where the fire had begun had burned themselves out, but nearby areas still burned brightly. The fire was spreading quickly, despite how much rain had fallen.

Arryn had instructed the Chieftain and Elysia to hold back on the rain they had conjured while she and the other magic users worked, so they could conserve their energy for when it would matter most. It had taken nearly two hours for Arryn, Amelia, Celine, the governor, and the other friendly physical magicians to reduce the fire enough for the water to begin to take effect.

The Chieftain, Elysia, and Cathillian stepped in then, calling on their combined powers to bring in a heavy, soothing rain.

"The ground will be made rich from the death here. No tree or animal will have perished in vain. Each one will feed the next generation, helping us to regrow this section of the Forest to be even stronger than it was before," the Chieftain had told them as the rains fell.

The birds, squirrels, and other small animals went to work bringing acorns and other seeds from the healthy parts of the forest and spreading them on the injured, but hungry earth before them.

Amelia, Celine, Samuel, and the natives of the other areas of the Valley watched in wonder. They never would have believed something like that could even be possible. It was like an oasis; every creature linked to the next by the druids they encountered every day.

There wasn't another place in Irth like it.

When they arrived back at the southern village, Arryn and Cathillian were sent to the river to tell the older druids and the children they had protected that it was safe to return home.

Arryn had never seen anything quite like the tiny barrier the children and the elderly had created. It was thicker and far stronger than the barrier protecting the internal parts of the Dark Forest where the druids resided.

Nothing would have gotten in.

Once the elderly had been filled in on what had happened and they had left with the children, Arryn took to the river, walking just far enough in that she could sit peacefully inside without being washed downstream.

She crossed her legs as she had in the Temple and closed her eyes, turning her nose to the still cloudy sky as she let what little sun poked through touch her.

"How are you doing?" Cathillian asked, interrupting her peace.

She sighed, silently motioning for him to join her. He sat next to her and reached for her hand, their eyes briefly meeting as she took it and wrapped her smaller fingers around his. Each wore the expression of someone who had lost much, but knew they could have lost so much more.

The look of someone who mourned what was gone as they struggled to allow themselves to see the light. It was there, but they both needed the time to accept what had happened.

Arryn's eyes closed again as she returned her gaze to the sky. "Why are you worried about me? This was your home before it was mine."

"I know that. I just... It's your home, too. Always has been. I think even back then—ever since the moment your mother brought you here with even a sliver of hope we could help—this was your home."

She gave him a sad smile while keeping her face to the sky. "Thank you. I needed that."

"You'll always have a home here, you know. You'll always have a home wherever I am. No matter what."

Tears filled her closed eyes. So much had happened in such a short time. Samuel coming into her life that day by the river had changed her world forever. She had grown in ways she hadn't even known possible.

It seemed that as soon as one journey ended the next would begin, and she had no idea how to handle it at times. But Cathillian had always been there to help her. He drove her crazy at times, but that had always been his way of distracting her.

There were moments when she wondered if he pissed her off on purpose just to keep her mind focused on something small and insignificant—like the anger she felt for him—instead of the larger, more threatening picture, like the one they faced now.

"I have to tell you something," he said, worry pulling at his voice. "I know you don't remember, and I know you'll be angry. It's okay to blame me, but I promise I didn't mean for it to happen."

The tears that burned her eyes fell from under her closed lids and spilled down her cheeks. She hadn't realized he had been carrying that kiss with him all this time with guilt. She knew what he was about to say, and it broke her heart for him to know he felt guilty for something she had done.

It was true that she hadn't remembered it initially, but Amelia had shown her what had happened. And even though she wished it hadn't happened as it did, and even though she would have preferred it wait for a time when she wasn't drunk out of her mind and war wasn't threatening them, she didn't regret it a bit. She didn't want him to either.

"I remember," she said, her voice weak from her tears.

His hand squeezed hers. "You do?"

She lifted their clasped hands from the water, bringing the back of his to her mouth and kissing it before lowering them back into the water.

She shook her head. "Please don't feel guilty. I don't."

Her throat tightened as she heard his breath catch, and her chest felt like it might explode. She couldn't process this. In her mind, she fought between this being the worst time possible for such a discussion, and the absolute best.

But Cathillian had brought it up, not her. As she sat there, trying to meditate but failing because her mind was so cluttered, she realized it didn't matter at that moment what confusion she felt. It wasn't all about her. He always considered *her* feelings— even now when his home had suffered so greatly and he had lost friends he had known since the day he was born.

After all that, he had still come to check on her. She wanted to be there for him.

Even if they were never to be anything more than friends, he was her very *best* friend, and he needed to know that she was okay. He needed to know *they* were okay.

As she thought that over, she realized now *was* the perfect time to discuss it—because her best friend needed to. It was the perfect time because they were about to be forced to put all losses

—from the forest, the men and women, and the animals—aside while they pressed on. While they went back into war to avenge those lost and those who would be still, and he needed to know.

She opened her eyes and looked into his. They were always a deep jade, but they seemed to shine right then, even in the low light.

"Yes. I remember. I didn't at first. Actually, Amelia showed me what happened. But once she did, it all came back." She paused as she watched his brows crease, worry on his face. "I wouldn't change that, Cathillian. Well, I wish I hadn't been in that condition, but otherwise I don't regret it at all."

He sighed heavily, a cautious smile on his face. "I was scared you were going to beat me."

She smiled. "Good man."

She felt his hesitation as he squeezed her hand once more before letting go. It seemed like there was more he wanted to say, but he was quiet—for once—as he faced the river again.

Taking a deep breath, Arryn rose to her knees and leaned toward him in a single fluid movement. His eyes widened as she placed her hand on the side of his face, turning him toward her.

Before she could do anything further, he wrapped his arms around her and tackled her to the ground, his lips finding hers. His long hair fell around them, and she ran her fingers through it as his hand gently caressed her side.

After he finally pulled away, he stared down into her eyes as he lifted his hand to stroke the side of her face, the pad of his thumb grazing her lower lip. "You have no idea how long I've wanted to do that."

She smiled. "It's good to know all those girls weren't full of shit."

His mouth fell open as his eyes widened, a deep laugh quickly finding him. "Damn. You sure know how to ruin a moment, don't you?"

She shrugged, smiling with him. "Hey, I'm just saying... I've had to listen to that for years. Not that I cared. 'Cause, you know, black heart and all."

He laughed again and she shifted, catching him by surprise as she threw him to the side before leaning over him and kissing him once more.

"And you're always surprising me. Especially that black heart of yours." He winked.

She sighed as she stared down at him. In that moment, she wasn't sure if she was grateful their time was limited, or if she hated the fact.

"I can tell by the look on your face that you're about to ruin all this," he said, still smiling as he brushed loose strands of her hair back over her ear.

She nodded. "I'm sorry. Look, I don't know about all this yet."

"Ah, here we go," he said, sitting up.

Laughing, she said, "No. No, it isn't like that. It's just... I've never once thought of myself as the type of girl to be with anyone. Certainly not my best friend."

He nodded. "I know that. It's why I've never said anything. But just so you know, this has been a thing since the day I met you."

She shook her head and sighed. "I had a feeling, but I always pushed it aside. I won't lie—it scares me a bit. Even more than running into Arcadia and starting a war."

He nodded. "I understand. How about we make a deal?"

"I'm listening," she said, eyeing him suspiciously.

"Once this is all over... Once Arcadia is back in Amelia's hands and we've defeated Alaric. Once all of that is settled, you and I will have a serious conversation about this. Whether it's you telling me you can't live without me or to fuck off and we're just friends. I don't care, as long as it's what will make you happy, and you take it seriously."

Her expression turned curious. "But if I decide something as girly as never being able to live without you, does that mean I can't tell you to fuck off anymore?"

He looked at her incredulously. "What? And deprive me of such sweet words? I would expect it."

She laughed. "Well, this is sounding better and better all the time. We really would make one messed-up pair."

He nodded. "I wouldn't have it any other way. Also... No. It's not girly to tell me you can't live without me. I would say it to *you*."

"*That's* your argument?" she asked, giving him the same incredulous look he had just given her.

He laughed. "Point taken. Clearly, I'm the prettier one in this relationship, and far more in tune with my feelings."

"Oh, Bitch," she said, laughing.

"But seriously—do we have a deal?"

"As long as nothing changes between us as far as our friendship goes, whether we become something more or not. You really are everything to me, and I don't want to lose our laughs. Plus, we enjoy insulting each other. You make it so easy."

"Done," he said.

They got to their feet, smiling as they sensed something moving through the trees across the river. Arryn stepped forward, her eyes changing to a deep obsidian as she prepared for an enemy to break through.

Instead, it was a little girl.

CHAPTER TWENTY-TWO

Arryn's eyes faded back to their natural color as the girl dropped down to the bank of the Kalt River. Her hair was a disheveled mess, and her dark skin had a hint of grey to it. From the greyish shade of her kinky hair and the color of her eyes, Arryn knew she was a dark druid child.

"Please," the girl said, raising her hands in a submissive manner. "Please let me cross the river. I came a long way, scared of what I'd find. But you're not bad. You're not like them. You don't deserve to die."

Arryn looked at Cathillian, and his eyes flashed green as he grew the weeds along the river to reach across the water. They gently wrapped around the girl's waist and pulled her to their side.

As he set her down, freeing her of what could have easily turned into her bonds, she smiled. "I'm different than you. I'm different than them, too, but you don't know me. All you know is that I look like your enemy, but you still trusted me." She smiled again. "You really *are* good."

Arryn smiled and knelt before the girl. She extended her hand, a look of shock crossing the girl's face before she cautiously placed her hand in Arryn's. "You can sense the good in others. You must be kind of like me. I always had a knack for reading people, too, and it's even stronger when I touch them."

The girl nodded, her smile growing. "That's the same with me. Sometimes, if someone is really bad or really good, I can sense it without needing to touch them. The druids who came to the Terres Forest are bad people. They plan to hurt you."

Arryn's brows creased. "You came all the way here to tell us this? To warn us?"

Cathillian kneeled then, too. "How old are you? Where are your parents?"

The little girl pulled her hand back, nervously picking at her filthy nails as her eyes turned toward the ground. She shook her head. "They don't like me. But that's okay, because I don't like them either. They're bad people. They hurt other people and take what they want. I'm only eight, and even *I* know that's not the way things are supposed to be."

That was one of the most horrifying things Arryn had ever heard. A child outcast not only among her people, but from her own parents. Family was everything, and without the people around her she had now, she never would've survived.

This girl was only a year younger than Arryn had been when she had come to the Dark Forest. *How fitting*, she thought, *that it be me the girl found first.*

"Are they coming the way you did? Straight through the Forest?" Cathillian asked.

The young dark druid shook her head, her matted curls bouncing as she did. "No. They planned to head south again, back to their land. They've got plans, but I think they'll be coming here soon enough."

Arryn felt chills as she realized just how much the girl had been through in her short life, not to mention the bravery it had taken for her to leave everything she had ever known to find people who were the enemy of her own. All that with nothing more than a glimmer of hope they might be better than where she came from.

Arryn scooted forward, giving her a comforting smile as she took both the girl's hands in her own. "How about we take you back to the village and introduce you to our Chieftain? If you like us, I can promise you'll like him. He's very funny, and he *loves* children. In fact, he pretty much *is* one."

The girl giggled, and Cathillian smiled as he said, "I can vouch for that. He's my grandfather, and sometimes he acts even younger than me. Hell, younger than *you*."

"After that, we'll all sit down and talk about what you saw and what you wanted to tell us. Then we'll get some food into your belly, and later I'll bring you back down here to the river and we'll get you cleaned up. I just know there's a beautiful girl under all this dirt," Arryn said with a smile.

The little girl nodded excitedly, and Arryn could sense her happiness. She had never been shown an ounce of acceptance, but that was about to change. Arryn decided right then that she would take responsibility for this girl, just as Elysia had done for her when she was child.

As THE SUN set on the Dark Forest, the scent of charred wood and oil still lingering in the air, Arryn and Elysia walked Corrine back to the village. It had taken them a long time, and Elysia had to help, but they had finally gotten the young girl's hair untangled and clean.

She looked like a brand-new kid. Her hair was beautiful and shiny. She had tight, kinky curls, and Arryn loved playing with them. There were other women in the village who had hair like hers, and Arryn couldn't wait to introduce her to them so they could teach her and Corrine how to properly care for it.

The Chieftain said the girl was from Jerick's tribe. While he hadn't gone to the extremes his brother Alaric had, he was still a very cruel man. That much was evident from the things Corrine had told them.

The Chieftain told them that although she had been born a dark druid, that didn't mean she was stuck as one. Over time, if she were fed properly and learned how to use more positive magic, the damage that had been done to her body would be cleansed.

As dark grey as her hair was, he had to assume it would turn to a rich, shiny black, and the grey tint to her skin would vanish, revealing a lovely dark healthy glow.

He was impressed the girl had been able to hold onto her soul while surrounded by people with such darkness. Corrine had immediately taken to the Chieftain, just as Arryn had hoped she would. She laughed at all his jokes, which only made the Chieftain like her more.

Arryn walked her back to her home, and Corrine was startled by what she saw waiting for them there.

"Oh, my," she said when she caught sight of Snow. "Will she bite me?"

Arryn laughed. "No. No familiar here will bite you. In fact, if you are ever in danger, any familiar in this village will give its life to save you. That's the way it should be. Human and animal alike —we're all family."

Corrine just stared at her for several moments before lunging forward and wrapping her arms around Arryn's waist. "Thank you."

And then, as if nothing had just happened, she turned and ran towards Snow, stopping just far enough away to be respectful. "Can I pet you? You look soft."

Arryn silently watched as Snow lowered her head, closing her eyes as she offered herself to the little girl.

"Do you want to play with me?" she asked excitedly as she ran her fingers through the tiger's fur.

Arryn laughed. "Snow isn't really the playful type, not that she doesn't like to. She just prefers to sleep. If you ever want snuggles, though, Snow is your girl. For playing, however…"

Arryn's eyes flashed for a moment as she reached out, searching for her cub, and within seconds she heard the pitter-patter of quick paws running at full speed toward them.

"This is Dante. All he ever does is play. Trees are his favorite, though I don't like him playing in them alone. He always gets stuck."

Dante skidded to a stop in front of the girl, giving her a cautious sniff before approaching with obvious excitement. Corrine reached out with both hands, petting him all over, which he gladly accepted as he flopped onto his back to demand belly rubs.

"I used to get stuck in trees all the time too, but I'm a lot better now. I'll show you how to get down!" Corrine said. "Come with me."

They ran to the closest tree that was suitable for climbing.

"How was it possible that someone didn't want that child?" Elysia asked as she walked up behind Arryn. "She's perfect."

Arryn nodded. "I get the feeling none of that matters, now that she's here. Not to her, anyway."

Elysia put her hand on the small of Arryn's back, giving her a gentle pat. "You're right. She's home now." Elysia sighed, a smile spreading on her lips.

"What is it?" Arryn asked.

"It's just amazing, you know. You and Cathillian finally realized the love you have for one another, and five seconds later you adopt a child together."

Arryn's jaw dropped and her eyes widened as she turned to Elysia. "*What did you just say?*"

Elysia laughed as they heard approaching footsteps. Arryn turned to see Cathillian coming toward them, and she directed her shocked expression toward him. His eyes widened in response.

"Shit!" he shouted, turning to run in the opposite direction. "Don't kill me!"

That made Elysia laugh even harder. "Oh, you have no idea how long I've waited for this. Don't be mad at him, child. He was excited and wanted to tell someone. You can't blame him, can you?"

"Logically? I suppose not. But we both know that I will find ways."

The Chieftain walked up behind them, placing his hands on their shoulders. "I hate to break this up, but the time has come. We need to meet around the fire and discuss what we plan to do in the morning. Because after a little rest, we're *all* marching on Arcadia."

Arryn and Elysia looked at one another briefly before turning back to the Chieftain, nodding in response. As he walked away, Arryn followed him, her brief moment of jokes and happiness gone as the weight of the impending war once again pressed down on her shoulders.

CHAPTER TWENTY-THREE

Amelia sat next to the fire with Samuel on one side and Celine on the other, watching as everyone filed in, ready to hear what the plan might be. A couple of familiar faces approached her.

"Elon!" Amelia said. "It's so nice to see you. You've been hidden away. Part of me wondered if you hadn't run altogether."

He had spent his time secluded from most everyone. She joked about thinking he had left, but she knew better. A couple of times, she had seen him sitting at the base of a tree in deep thought—more than likely thinking of his son Gregory. She had to imagine if he'd had parchment with him, he would have designed many incredible inventions by then.

He shook his head. "Never. Not until this is finished." He gestured to the man standing to his left. His mentor, Waylon. "We have something for you. Or I guess I should say, *he* has something for you."

"When did you get here?" Amelia asked, standing to greet the engineer with a smile.

He returned her smile. "I have eyes and ears all over that city. I have had them since Adrien was in power. But when they stopped coming around, I knew something was wrong. You confirmed as much when you came to see me, but it got worse. I decided to get out and do some digging of my own, and I overheard two guardsmen talking about Arryn. They were talking about planning an attack on the Dark Forest, so I left that night."

Amelia nodded. "I suppose with all the excitement, we've been pretty scattered. So, what do you have for us?"

Elon wore a large bag on his back, which he carefully brought around and set on the ground. He opened it and pulled a box free, handing it to Amelia. She gently opened it to see a round disc-like object inside. Her eyes lifted toward Elon again.

"Don't worry," he said. "They're not active. A switch on the bottom engages it. Once flipped, it would need to be placed in the ground to work properly. Just make sure you set it down *carefully* to keep the charges from detonating."

Waylon smiled again. "I recommend digging the hole, then using magic to set the charge. Levitate it in there. Human hands are very shaky things when scared."

"I know you wanted these to protect against a remnant invasion, but they might come in handy in the war to come. You guys are planning to march on Arcadia. There are a couple of thousand guards in there. You know as well as I do that not everyone will get out alive. If it's between you—the people trying to save the city—and a dozen or more men getting ready to take your heads and prevent you from doing it, you throw that damn charge and let it take them," Elon said.

Amelia smiled. "Be careful, Elon. I might just start to think we're becoming friends."

"Why the hell would we do a fool thing like that?" he asked sarcastically. "But seriously—watch your back. If an army of men and women threaten to keep you from doing what you came to do, then do whatever it takes."

Closing the box, Amelia set it back in the bag before walking over and giving Elon a hug. "Thank you. Both of you." She pulled away, making eye contact with the man she had once hated but had now come to respect. "You've made a lot of mistakes, but you've gone to great lengths to make amends for them. Your son would be proud of you. I think we both know him well enough to know that."

Elon pursed his lips as he nodded. He reached out and gave her shoulder a gentle squeeze before turning and walking away, taking Waylon with him.

"Elon," Amelia said, stopping both Elon and his mentor. "Why don't both of you get some food? Join us for the evening."

Both engineers smiled, Elon nodding before they made their way over to get some wine.

When the dust had settled from the battles they would face, Amelia knew that she couldn't just arrest him again. She couldn't stand the thought of putting him back into a cell to rot.

The man had made many, many mistakes, but he was determined to right them. It wasn't her place to forgive what he had done to Gregory, but it *was* in her power to forgive him for betraying the city. After all he had done to help her protect it, she felt a pardon was warranted.

As long as things with Elon continued in such a positive way, the only thing she could think to do that was befitting was to free him. Let him find his son. If Gregory chose to let the past stay in the past, Elon would be able to live a happy life with his son. If not—well, Amelia imagined he would accept that and continue to pay for those wrongs.

Deep down, Amelia hoped for the best. She wanted to see him reconnect with his son.

Everyone gathered around the fire as the Chieftain approached. Instead of the happy expression he usually wore, this one showed only sadness and anger.

"I know everyone feels lost right now. I know everyone feels the weight of what's to come. We're all in this together. Each and every one of us has something special to contribute to this fight, and we will need those contributions in order to win. Now, Arryn, Amelia, and even Samuel know the city better than anyone, so tonight I'm passing the responsibility of planning our strategy to them. We should all listen and do what we do best—offer counsel where it's needed."

Amelia smiled at Arryn as the young woman took a step forward, accepting the position the Chieftain had granted her with great aplomb. Amelia looked at Samuel and he nodded, and together they stood to join their friend by the fire in hopes of creating a plan that would gain them the city and allow them to end Scarlett for good.

AFTER NEARLY RIDING their horses into the ground, Scarlett, her magicians, and the Arcadian Guard had reached the city walls in only a day and a half. They knew they would need any time they had gained in the fast ride to recover and to create a plan.

Without a doubt, Scarlett knew the druids would be upon them almost immediately. Possibly in as little as a few hours, though she imagined it might be a bit longer, given the effort they would have had to expend to put out the fires.

She had thought Arryn's intervention was a possibility, but not quite to the extent it had happened. She had made the mistake of believing she had adequately prepared for such an occurrence—but she had been very mistaken.

Not only had she been wrong in her initial assumption that they were outside the druids' range, but she had also been wrong about the time they had left before Arryn's return.

How could she have been so stupid? Why did she not think about the animals warning the druids?

She realized it was because she didn't understand nature magic in the least, and certainly hadn't given it the respect it deserved.

Now, the threat of losing everything she had worked for and exhausted herself over for so long was upon her. She couldn't let Arryn win. Not like this.

Nikolai walked into Scarlett's office, a bottle of whiskey in his hand. "I think you need something a little stronger than the brew."

She nodded, extending her hand to accept the bottle. She didn't even bother with a glass, just pulled out the stopper and brought it to her mouth. "How many of our own did we lose?"

"We lost Jonathan and Zara," Nikolai said, a twinge of sadness in his voice.

Scarlett thought for a few moments, trying to remember their faces. "Which ones were they?"

"Zara had the fiery red hair, and Jonathan had a shaved head. How do you not know these people? You were the one who recruited them."

She waved a hand in the air. "No, I said that I sent for *friends*. Those friends sent other friends, and I didn't realize that until they arrived. The only one I bothered remembering was Lacy, and that was only because she just happened to be your sister. Kade was rather attractive, so I remembered him as well."

Nikolai shook his head as he smiled. "Well, minus my sister, they're all expendable. That's the good news."

Scarlett sighed as she stared at the bottle. "What should we do? I need counsel more now than ever."

"Relax. Right now, we're rallying the Guard. The *full* Guard. We aren't wasting any resources this time. From what Barbara and Lacy have told me, things are going well."

Scarlett laughed. "Clearly, you and I have *wildly* different opinions about what 'going well' means. Didn't you see what was happening out there? The druids weren't killing the guardsmen. The druids knew *not* to kill them. Arryn was turning them right and left. Our hold on them was so frail that a simple knock to the head brought them out of it."

CANDY CRUM & MICHAEL ANDERLE

"That may be so, but they will be scarred for quite some time. We can easily get back in. We've been working on these people for a very long time, and the effects of that won't disappear overnight."

Scarlett sighed. "No, but the direct control we have over them will. Those men saw her taking others out right and left—breaking their legs or just knocking them out to keep from killing them—which wasn't what we've been telling them to see. They didn't see a cold-blooded murderer. Even when they came at her in the heat of battle with swords and knives, she couldn't bring herself to kill them. That made them wonder why in the hell she would have snuck into the city, broken into the barracks, and slit the throats of several guards in their sleep if she wouldn't even use a blade in battle. She used a *staff*, for fuck's sake."

Nikolai sat there, quietly considering her words. It was obvious he had no idea how to respond to that.

"Exactly," Scarlett said, taking another drink. "I want scouts to surround the city. With the druids to the west and the threat of the remnant to the east, we can't afford a single mistake."

His eyes widened for a moment before a look of guilt crossed his face.

"What is it?" she asked in an exasperated tone.

"I completely forgot. I'm so sorry. As I was on my way in here, a guard stopped me to report that a scout spotted the remnant marching this way."

Scarlett's jaw fell open slightly in shock. "This can't be happening. It doesn't even matter *how* it happens. We're *fucked*! If the remnant arrive first, they'll kill countless guardsmen before the druids even get here. If the druids arrive first I'm sure most of the men will survive, but they will take the city."

Nikolai swallowed hard, nodding. "And if they arrive at the same time…"

Scarlett shivered. "Keep your damn fear to yourself. Trust me, I've already thought about that." She exhaled deeply, rubbing the bridge of her nose. "Set up a perimeter on the eastern and western walls. Make sure no less than one hundred guardsmen are waiting at the gate. Place bowmen and magicians along the wall."

"Uh," he started nervously, "during the time I've spent with the Guard, I've learned there really aren't any bowmen. Before Arryn was run out of the city, she had been training a few, but most of them were the ones that she was able to turn against us on the field."

Scarlett shot him an angry look. "Then double the magicians on the walls, you idiot. Think!"

Nikolai was visibly hurt by her statement, but he blew it off, nodding in response before taking his leave. Scarlett took another long drink from the bottle, then put the stopper back in and set it down.

Any more than that and she would be drunk, unable to focus. As it was she was beginning to feel relaxed, and that was exactly what she would need while preparing for Arryn.

As she stared at the floor, her eyes drawn to the bloodstain where Talia's head had rested, she couldn't help but think about Arryn coming for her. Scarlett smiled. "May the best bitch win."

CHAPTER TWENTY-FOUR

A rryn and Snow slowed down as they approached the Arcadian border. Arryn could see guardsmen along the western wall of the city, and she could only imagine there were more waiting inside.

Their approach had to be perfect. Like last time, they would be fighting men who didn't deserve to die for someone who not only didn't give a damn about them, but had put them in that position to begin with.

She wished the Cellan Guard was with them, knowing some of them had at least a working knowledge of physical magic and were well trained. But it was too dangerous to leave the Forest unguarded, so the Chieftain—shockingly—had asked them to stay behind while he and the rest sought revenge for the death and destruction Scarlett had caused.

The governor had wanted to come along, but knowing what it was like to want revenge for their home being destroyed, he agreed—giving his word no harm would come to the druid people while he was there.

"Are you ready for this?" Elysia asked.

Still focused on the men ahead, Arryn nodded. "Absolutely. Let's go."

Everyone broke into a run, their horses or familiars carrying them as fast as they possibly could. Given how many warriors they had with them, Arryn knew the guards would be worried. As they approached, she saw that she had been right.

The men outside the wall sprinted for the gate the moment they saw the druid army approaching, obviously hoping to get to shelter before their enemy reached them.

But that wouldn't save them.

The Chieftain lifted his fingers to his mouth, letting out an ear-piercing whistle. Birds quit circling overhead and flew directly over the city. Each one carried a seed of some tree variety, most of them acorns.

The group rounded the southern edge of the city. As they headed toward the now-closed gate, Arryn watched the birds dropping the seeds onto the main street.

Magicians had been stationed on top of the walls and began throwing fireballs at them as they approached. Arryn, Amelia, Celine, and a few others moved to the front to keep the fire from hitting anyone. Their eyes turned black as they used their own power to deflect the fireballs as they came.

Before they got too close, Arryn stopped Snow, dismounting along with Cathillian as they made their way to the gate. They briefly looked at one another before nodding, their eyes flashing green as they lifted their arms to the side and then thrust their hands forward.

A blast of wind hit the gate hard, breaking it apart and blowing it all the way in. Amelia and Celine stepped toward the guardsmen standing with their magitech rifles lifted, their eyes turning black as they erected a large shield between the magitech rifles and their warriors.

The Chieftain, Elysia, and several other druids, their eyes

glowing green, lowered themselves to the ground. They placed their hands in the grass, and the ground began to shake.

Inside the city, rocks crumbled or split with sounds like shots as the growing root systems tore apart the cobblestone streets. The seeds had begun to sprout.

The guardsmen looked around, frantically trying to see what was happening. Within moments, the seeds the birds had dropped from overhead had grown into large, sturdy trees. They grew even larger as more druids dropped to the ground, adding their power.

The Arcadians watched in shock as the collective power of the druids overgrew their main street with trees.

Once they were large enough, the Chieftain stood and shouted, "*Schatten!*"

Vines burst from the ground as the *Schatten* warriors ran forward. They wrapped around their waists as the druids' magic manipulated the vines to thrust them over the stunned guardsman and into the newly-grown branches.

Loud yells came from the east just as the guardsmen regained their wits, and began firing their rifles at the druid warriors outside the gate. Each shot was deflected by Celine and Amelia's shield.

"What's that screaming?" Amelia shouted. "Please tell me that isn't what I think it is. Because what it sounds like to me..."

Arryn broke formation, striding off to the side where she could see, but was still protected by the shield. "Uh, if you think it's a massive hoard of remnant, you're *not* wrong."

"I think you were supposed to tell her that it *wasn't* what she thought it was," Cathillian said.

"Oh!" Arryn said, walking back to Amelia and Celine. "In that case, no. It's not an angry horde of remnant. But if it *were*, it's possible that we should get the *fuck* out of the way. Maybe now."

The Chieftain turned to Arryn. "We need the Guard. There

are ten times as many of them coming over that hill as there are of us."

More fireballs rained down on them from the wall. It shocked Arryn that they would still attack them instead of turning their attention to the invading remnant. Then again, the remnant were still too far out to reach easily.

Arryn's eyes turned black as she swung her arm to the side, deflecting the fireballs toward the oncoming horde.

"I think it's time for one of your famous speeches," Cathillian advised.

Arryn nodded and allowed her power to swell around her, pushing against her in all directions before it imploded. She disappeared from where she stood behind the shield and reappeared on the wall next to several magicians.

"Whoa, whoa, whoa!" Arryn shouted as she held up her hands. "Stop this! There is a *fucking horde of remnant* coming this way. What you don't realize is that we are *not* here to kill you. But they are! We're here to kill Scarlett—the mystic who has been controlling all of you."

"Arryn!" Cathillian shouted. "Maybe you should talk a little faster."

Arryn turned to the army of guardsmen standing on the ground below, their magitech rifles aimed at her now. "You Arcadians can choose to fight *us*, the people who haven't tried to kill *any* of you—even on the battlefield. Or you can fight *with* us against the remnant. Because I *promise* you, they're here for Scarlett, and they will rip every one of you to pieces just to get to her."

Arryn looked around as they turned to one another and considered their words. A few hesitantly nodded while others stood quiet, taking their lead from the others.

Arryn turned to the druid warriors on the ground. "Druids! To the trees! Everyone else, get inside the city."

Vines began shooting from the ground as the druid army advanced into the trees they had grown. Arryn turned toward the

Arcadian Guard inside the gate. "Retreat farther into the city! Let the remnant come inside."

"Are you sure you're on our side?" a magician on the wall behind her asked. That very magician had been one of her coworkers when she had taught at the Academy.

Arryn turned to face her. "The safest place for any Arcadian to be is underneath those trees. We're going to fight using the exact same tactics that we came here to use on Arcadia, only this time we won't use it against *you*. Understand?"

Someone shouted her name from the ground, and she saw Celine and Amelia below. Several magicians on the wall used their power to levitate them to the top, much to Arryn's surprise.

"Thank you, Cheryl," Amelia said.

"Chancellor," Cheryl acknowledged with a curt nod.

"Amelia, you call the shots from up here on the wall. I'm going to stay on the ground with Snow and Cathillian," Arryn said. "If the Arcadian Guard see all of us fighting to keep them alive, maybe we can take back the city without lifting a finger against them."

Amelia nodded. "Go *now*! They're coming."

Arryn smiled before jumping to the ground and rushing over to the terrified guards. They had started backing farther into the city, hands shaking as they held swords or rifles in front of them.

She heard Amelia shouting orders just before the flashes of fire began. Those were quickly followed by the screams of remnant.

"Druids, here they come! Ready yourselves," Arryn shouted into the trees.

"Arryn," Cathillian and Elysia both screamed, and Cathillian continued, "What the hell are you doing? Get your ass up here!"

She shook her head. "In case you hadn't noticed, I'm the only thing keeping these men from running. This horde is at least twice the size of the last one that came for the city. They're scared to death, and I'm not leaving them."

Arryn turned her head back toward the gate as someone jumped down next to her. It was Cathillian, and Elysia quickly jumped down on her other side.

Cathillian winked at her, giving a brief smile. "Don't act so shocked. We still need to have that talk, and I intend to see you don't do anything to get out of it. You know, like dying."

"Damn, that was my plan," Arryn replied. "The easy way out."

Cathillian only smiled and rolled his eyes in response.

The remnant ran through the gate, their hideous faces angry. Some of them had been terribly burned, but it was obvious that the flames had had little effect on them as they ran full-speed toward their group.

Arryn stepped forward, her eyes turning black as she lifted her arms out by her sides. Rocks both large and small lifted from the cobblestone street as she thrust them forward.

The smaller rocks landed hard enough to break the skin, penetrating not unlike arrows. The larger ones beat them unmercifully, throwing some of them back while others fought to keep running despite the pain.

Vines began whipping through the air again as the druids in the trees lassoed the remnant and pulled them into the trees. Their plan was to grab enough to disperse the initial wave.

Arryn pulled her blades from the sheaths on the back of her belt and shouted for her familiar. "*Snow!*"

To her surprise, the tiger was not the only one to show. Zobig ran forward with the big cat, both hurtling full force into the crowd of remnant and further breaking it apart.

"Go!" Cathillian shouted as he raised his sword to the sky.

The men and women of the Guard and the druid warriors on the ground ran forward, cutting remnant down as the beasts ran into the city.

As expected, the trees were enough to break the horde into smaller groups, since they were forced to move around them. Those clusters got even smaller as the druids above pulled some of them into the trees. They were further scattered by the enormous familiars barreling through their ranks.

So far, the plan was working exactly as expected.

"Stay low, lass," Samuel offered before thrusting his hammer upward into the jaw of a remnant, dropping him before smashing his skull.

Arryn did as the rearick said, ducking and running through the monstrous warriors. She ripped holes in their bellies or hamstrung them before slicing their throats. It was a brilliant technique, and one that was working for her and Samuel.

The remnant were focused on the enemies in front of them, too shortsighted to look down.

But even so, this wasn't the target she had planned to fight.

She had yet to see Scarlett, which meant the bitch was more than likely hiding somewhere. Arryn knew she couldn't battle the horde forever, but she still needed to make sure the initial plan they had made was keeping everyone safe.

Arryn started fighting her way backward through the more widely scattered remnant. A young guard had been cornered by three of them. Judging from the look on his face, he didn't have any confidence in his own abilities, so she didn't take any chances.

Arryn threw one of her daggers, hitting the center one in the side of the neck as she ran full speed for the one on the left. As that remnant swung his sword Arryn leapt into the air, tumbling once to avoid the blade before wrapping her legs around his neck.

She flung her weight backward as hard as she could, put her hands down for stability, and effectively flipped him over her. As soon as he landed, she tightened her legs and twisted, breaking his neck.

She heard the footsteps before she saw the next attacker, her eyes turning black as she flexed her entire body. A shield burst forth, protecting her as the remnant brought his axe down.

Metal crashed against the shield, Arryn gritting her teeth as she used all the strength she could muster to push the shield against the blade to gain any distance she could. She twisted the fingers of her free hand to pull water from the humid air, instantly making her throat scratchy.

With a loud grunt, Arryn shoved her shield forward as hard as she could, throwing him back just far enough that she was able to drop it. As he raised his axe again, Arryn thrust her hand forward, the water immediately freezing as the jagged ice spear shot forward, impaling him through the face.

Groaning in disgust, Arryn rolled out from under the remnant whose neck she had broken and climbed to her feet as the other fell dead. She looked at the young guardsman she had just saved. "You okay?"

The guard nodded in response, clearly unable to speak at that moment.

"If you can't fight, find a place to hide. There's no shame in that, if you think you'll cost someone their life. But if you have the courage, do your best to save someone. Stick to the outside of the battle and find the stragglers. Catch them one at a time, and you'll be fine."

Arryn, I can sense her. She's close, Zoe sent telepathically. *She's been watching.*

Arryn punched a remnant in the gut as he ran for her, then thrust her knee into his groin. As he fell to his knees, she grabbed the knife from his belt and jammed it through the back of his neck, severing his spine. She let go of his knife and ran to the other remnant she had just killed to retrieve her blades.

Zoe, come with me. I'm going to need you for this, Arryn replied.

CHAPTER TWENTY-FIVE

C athillian caught up with Samuel, and the two paired up to fight next to one another, combining forces. Cathillian figured the rearick could use the help, because he couldn't stop checking the wall to make sure Celine was still okay.

More remnant poured through the front gate even though the magicians rained fire on them, and Cathillian had another idea. The devices made Amelia nervous, but Cathillian knew they were necessary right then.

"Samuel, will you be okay down here?" Cathillian asked as he turned to run his sword through the belly of a remnant. Samuel, a good partner, struck him in the back of the head with his hammer.

"Abandonin' me already, are ye?" he replied, dropping to his knees and hitting a remnant in the gut with his hammer before rolling out of the way. Cathillian swung downward and took the beast's head off.

"That depends. Do you think Amelia should use those charges Elon created now, or do you want to continue fighting these bastards by the wave?"

Both men ran toward a very large remnant, slightly taller than even Cathillian. Samuel dropped to the ground and slid between the monster's legs before rolling to his feet behind him.

That action distracted him long enough for Cathillian to cut him down as the rearick turned to smash a remnant in the side of the head.

"As much fun as I'm havin' dancin' with ye down here, lad, I've gotta say she needs ta get off her scared little arse with those things and use them," he replied.

Cathillian took out another remnant and ran into a nearby alley, where he climbed to the roof of the nearest building. Jumping from roof to roof until he neared the wall, he used a vine to swing from the final roof to the top of the wall.

He began making his way through the magicians, happy that none of them were paying him a bit of attention. Arryn had put them in their place, but he had no delusions that everything was fine between them.

He had no trust for Arcadians right then, not until Scarlett and the others were gone. They had simply chosen the path of least resistance. He wouldn't put it past them to attack him, Arryn, or the other warriors from the Dark Forest once they were safe from the remnant.

"Hey," Cathillian said when he finally reached Amelia. "I can't help but notice you have this handy little bag here, and the contents are still inside."

"You have any idea what those things do?" Amelia asked as she thrust her hands forward, sending several remnant flying into the stone wall surrounding the city. Their heads split on impact.

"Amelia, you're exhausted. I can see it, and I can even *feel* it radiating off you. Your energy levels are low. There are many more remnant coming, and you've given damn near all you had to give. Let me help you."

She looked at him, her black eyes hollow and the rings dark around them. She was pale, and he could tell she had already gone beyond what she was safely capable of giving.

He reached out and grabbed her wrist, letting some of his magic flow into her. He didn't give her much—he would need it for the battle below—but it was still enough to put a little bit of life back into her.

"Thank you," she said. "You really want to hold those things while they're active?"

"You commissioned these to be built, and they're gonna save our asses now as well as keep the city safe later."

Cathillian liberated a box from the bag. He pulled it free and held his hands over the railing, balancing the device on the fingertips of one hand as he flipped the switch on the bottom with the other.

"The pressure plate is in the center, raised above the rest. You can touch the outsides without anything happening," he said, pulling his arm back and throwing the magitech mine as hard as he could.

Amelia extended her hand to manipulate the device's landing. Once it was on the ground, a remnant stepped on it within a second or two.

The first blast took out several remnant in the immediate area. A few seconds later another charge went off, killing at least ten more who had been stupid enough to come close.

"Holy Bitch!" Amelia shouted.

Cathillian cheered excitedly. "Elon's a *fucking* genius!"

Amelia turned to Cathillian with a smile on her face. "Can you get us to the other side of the wall with those? They will detonate ten times before needing to cool down. After they're cool they'll detonate ten more times, and they'll continue the cycle until the crystal burns out. We could probably wipe out most of them—at least those that are stupid enough to continue on the same path."

Cathillian nodded. "We'll stagger them so we can hit more of them."

Amelia gave quick orders to the magicians on the wall, instructing them to conserve their power as much as possible, but to do their best to keep the remnant separated. Once she finished speaking, she and Cathillian made their way across the destroyed gate with the help of his magic before running down the wall to locate a good spot from which to throw the first charge.

"Thank you for this," Amelia said. "Having them explained to you while looking at the diagram on parchment and actually holding one in your hand are very different. One sounds fun and exciting, but the other is terrifying."

He gave her a smile and a wink as he reached into the bag and pulled another box free. "Well, let's have some fun now. Here we go!"

ELYSIA TOOK to the trees again as soon as the Guard proved they were capable of fighting the remnant. They weren't skilled, but it would suffice. She had her own people to attend to and check on. As she lifted herself into a tree she saw her druids all over, using their magic to move the branches and manipulate the roots.

The remnant below were pulled into the trees, smashed with roots, or killed by diving *Schatten*. It was the exact same method they had planned to use against the Arcadian Guardsman, though for that application the instruction had been to pull the men into the trees and subdue them—not kill them.

"Is everyone okay up here?" Elysia asked.

Ryel jumped to the branch she stood on and gave her a salute. "Everything has gone according to what we talked about. We've lost three, but we've taken far more remnant lives than that."

Losing anyone at all didn't sit well with Elysia, but as far as battles and war went, that was not only an acceptable number, it was actually good.

She nodded. "My father's still on the ground, and Cathillian is on the wall with Amelia. I haven't seen Arryn in a while, Have any of you?"

Alehah jumped down in front of them. Given the things that had happened in the Forest, Elysia and her father had felt it would be good if the former *Schatten* were there to help. It would allow her to use her abilities and get that out of her system while also seeing the consequences of her actions. Elysia herself was dealing with that same lesson.

Alehah saluted her Elder before speaking. "I saw Arryn earlier fighting her way farther into the city. We've grown more trees along the way, and we spread out more once the remnant moved farther inside."

Elysia sighed. "She must be going for Scarlett. I can't let her do this alone."

The girl nodded. "She has the young mystic with her. I'll retrieve Rae for you. Is there anyone else you'd like to go with you? Clara and Cassondra are close."

Elysia's eyes widened. She hadn't even thought about Clara. She could prove to be very useful, especially when they needed subtlety.

Nodding, Elysia said, "Excellent choices. I'm heading back to the ground, since all of you are safe. I need to check on the Arcadians to make sure they aren't dying right and left. Arryn didn't exaggerate at all—these men and women *are* poorly trained."

"Perhaps that's something we could all address once the city is back in capable hands?" Alehah suggested with an inflection at the end, making it a subtle question.

It suddenly occurred to Elysia that she had befriended the woman rightfully in charge of the city. There was no longer a need to feel disdain towards the city or its people. They had been taught their entire lives that it was okay to do whatever was necessary, as long as they stayed on top. Amelia was a good woman, and Elysia had faith she would instill better values.

After all she had done to keep Cathillian and Arryn safe when she herself could not, Elysia felt she owed Amelia something. Elysia didn't think Amelia would accept repayment, since she herself wouldn't. But if she were to offer a service—something that would make her city stronger—perhaps Amelia would allow it.

"I think that conversation needs to happen," Elysia said. "You're more than welcome to join me for it."

Alehah straightened then, cautious excitement and pride in her expression as she saluted one last time. Elysia left the tree, heading back down to check on the guardsmen while Alehah retrieved the warriors she had named.

Arryn was going to need help. Elysia sure as hell wasn't going to let her do this one alone.

CHAPTER TWENTY-SIX

With Zoe at her side, Arryn had fought her way through the thinner groups of remnant that had scattered farther into the city. They were searching for Scarlett, but Arryn wasn't about to let them take the mystic—not after what she had done to the Dark Forest.

"Do you still sense her?" Arryn asked.

Zoe nodded. "I do. Unfortunately, I sense more than her. There are four more mystics in the area, and none of them feel friendly."

Arryn nodded. "Fantastic."

"I hear that animals are quite useful," Elysia said as she approached from behind. Arryn turned and smiled when she saw her. "You know, I expected to find a fight or two that would slow me down."

Arryn scrunched her face and shook her head in amusement. "Nah. Zoe and I had all the fun before you showed up."

Elysia laughed. "Yeah, I can see that."

"What were you saying about animals?" Arryn asked.

Elysia cleared her throat, a momentary look of guilt crossing her face. "While you were gone to the Heights, I snuck into the city to get information. Long story short, things went bad, and I and the shadow warriors with me got into a fight with the mystics. In the end, we used the city's animals to our advantage. The mystics can't affect their minds, only humans. When we realized we were seeing things the animals weren't, we were able to fight past the illusions."

Zoe nodded. "Actually, that's brilliant. I've never fought beside druids before, so I hadn't thought of that as an option, but that will give you an excellent advantage. Both of you have strong minds, and Arryn, I know from personal experience that your mental barrier has gotten much better. If you use the animals as your eyes and allow yourself to really get into their heads, the mystics will have a much harder time getting in yours."

"What about the remnant? They're kind of human. Well, not exactly. I don't really know how to describe what they are," Arryn said.

Shaking her head, Zoe said, "We have books that say the remnant aren't like humans. Their minds are fundamentally different, though there's no way for us to know. With Julianne in the Madlands, it's possible she might know, but I'm sure as hell not going near them. I doubt even Scarlett would be able to control them. The only worry we have is her gaining control over any of us."

Arryn felt a familiar buzzing in the back of her mind, a dull thrum of energy pressing on her as someone began fishing. "Is that you?"

"No. She knows we're here," Zoe replied.

As her words sank in, Arryn felt a backhanded tap against her hip. She quickly turned to see Elysia staring forward, the woman jabbing her chin in the direction she stared.

Arryn turned to look in the direction Elysia had pointed, and saw her prize.

"Hello, hello!" Scarlett said with an almost excited tone in her voice. The mystic had every bit of the excitement in her eyes that Arryn had heard in her voice.

With a smile, Arryn said, "Aw, well, I'm glad you're as happy as we are that today's the day you die. That saves me a *lot* of worry, lemme tell ya."

Scarlett laughed. "I'm going to miss that sense of humor. You really do have a good one. We'll see how great that sense of humor is after I've turned your brain to soup."

Arryn could feel the mystic pressing against her mind as she tested her shield. *She would have to try harder than that.*

"You've gotten much better! Very nice. It won't save you, though. You poor child! It *was* rather sad that you never found that father of yours. I'll have to send him your head, though I'd bet he wouldn't give a damn."

"Don't let her rattle you," Zoe whispered. "She's trying to shake your resolve and weaken your barrier. She has no idea where your father is. It's because she's too weak to get in herself." The last sentence had been said at a higher volume to emphasize her point to Scarlett.

The mystic laughed and shook her head. "It's really cute you brought a baby mystic with you. Again—not gonna save ya, gorgeous."

Arryn could feel that her familiar was close, but she couldn't see her. Risking a look through Snow's eyes, she saw that the big cat was slinking behind buildings that weren't far away from where they were now.

She smiled as she pulled back into her own head, knowing the tiger had something planned. She only had to stall for a little while longer.

"You know, I would *love* to stand around and chat all day," Arryn said, "but how about we get this going? We've got some shit to move back into Amelia's office, and I needed to get some things from my house." Arryn gave a chuckle as she extended her arms to her side. "There's just *so* much to do, and not enough time! I'm sure you understand."

Scarlett nodded, her smile never fading. "You know, I always found your blasé attitude toward your position rather humorous when directed at Talia. It always made me laugh, even if I had to do it on the inside so she couldn't hear me. But now that it's directed at me, I have to say it's pretty fucking annoying. You should learn your place."

"Ha! You mean, like me accepting that I would be unable to escape the Frozen North? Should I have bowed to Talia, the bitch whose life I splattered all over the floor in that office you like to *think* is yours? Which place should I learn, Scarlett? Because from where I'm standing, it's *you* who has a misunderstanding of just where she belongs."

Scarlett opened her mouth to respond, but closed it again. Arryn had put her at a loss for words, which only seemed to infuriate her more.

"She just called to the others," Zoe said.

"How do you know? Can you see into her head?" Arryn whispered back.

Zoe nodded, her eyes slightly surprised. "She's weaker than usual, but don't let that be a comfort. She's strong. *Really* strong."

"She'd have to be," was all Arryn responded with as guardsmen began to fill the street.

They were still clearly under the control of the four mystics who had just entered the large open area.

"Let's see you get out of *this* one with that soul of yours intact," Scarlett said.

Another image sent by Snow told her the cat only needed a little more time. Arryn couldn't risk looking for too long to see what the tiger had planned, but she trusted her completely.

"Non-lethal blows," Arryn said.

"I'll try to free a couple if I can," Zoe said.

Guards charged at them, and Arryn engaged. When the first guard swung his sword, she ducked low before punching him in the ribs. She then dropped to her knees, spinning so her back was to him as she pulled one of her daggers and stabbed backward into his outer thigh, doing her best to avoid hitting his femoral artery.

When he cried out and doubled over, she reached up, wrapping her arms around his neck before flipping him over her shoulders onto the ground in front of her.

She tumbled out of the way of another guard, rolling onto her knees and sweeping his legs. His knees buckled as he landed and Arryn hit him in the face with the hilt of her dagger, knocking him unconscious before she retrieved the other dagger from the leg of the first man.

Zoe attacked with her staff and Elysia went hand-to-hand, as Arryn had. Each of them worked hard to take the innocent men down without casualties, but it proved to be difficult since the mystics pushed them to be even more fearless and violent.

A guard managed to land a blow across Arryn's face as another stabbed her through the back, the blade coming out through her stomach.

Suddenly, they began screaming and falling to the ground. Before Arryn could figure out what had happened, the sword was pulled free of her back and a warm hand was on her shoulder, sending heat through her body.

"It's almost over," Elysia said.

Arryn stared at the overwhelmed and now unconscious bodies of the guards, knowing Zoe had done it to save her. At first, Arryn had thought she killed them, but she had only made them pass out.

"Yes," Arryn said, her voice low and icy. "It's almost over."

When the wounds had closed, Arryn got to her feet, her eyes turning obsidian and green.

"Arryn," Elysia warned. "Be careful."

Zoe shook her head at Elysia as Arryn crossed her path. "She's in control. Let her go."

"Oh!" Scarlett said with an amused expression. "What's all this? You look like you might be a bit irritated."

Wind had begun to swirl around Arryn, her long dark braid whipping her back.

Elysia and I will take the others. Scarlett is yours, Zoe sent.

Arryn nodded as she took a step forward. "It's time to end this," she spat.

"I couldn't agree more," Scarlett replied.

The mystic's smile fell the moment her eyes flashed white. Inside her mind, Arryn felt the barrier she had worked so hard to hold crumble like it was made of sand as the mystic slammed into her.

Pain seized her entire body, and she began to shake—her chest suddenly felt as if it were on fire. Struggling to remain standing, she looked down and saw a charred hole, with blood pouring from the wound.

The Hunter standing several feet away was holding a magitech rifle that had recently been fired. She had seen him somewhere before, but it took a few moments for it to hit her. When it did, the world around her began to spin. Her body was still upright somehow, though she couldn't understand why.

"Recognize him, do you?" Scarlett asked. "He killed your mother—but you knew that, didn't you? Look down, girl. You now bear the very wound you left your mother to die with. Fitting you should go in the same way she did. She was a worthless piece of shit. *A traitor*. And she gave birth to a traitor."

Arryn struggled to move her hands to the wound in her chest, and her knees buckled as she fell. She couldn't speak or cry out. She could only feel intense pain, the same pain her mother must have felt.

She died because of you, Scarlett told her telepathically, her magic lending a bit of influence to truly drive the point.

"N-no," Arryn finally forced out.

Scarlett laughed as Elysia's and Zoe's screams filled Arryn's ears. She wanted to see what was happening, but she couldn't move.

"No?" Scarlett laughed again. "Oh, honey. It's *adorable* you believe that. Had you been a better student—a better *daughter* —you could have stood together to fight. Instead, she had to protect you. I can see everything you hide in that twisted little brain of yours, Arryn.

"You never paid attention to your mother during lessons. You wanted to *play* instead of learn anything, didn't you? She had to fight you to spend time with her at all. Look what it cost her! She raised an ungrateful little bitch, and you're *still* ungrateful. That druid boy loves you and would die to protect you, yet you can't even tell him the truth. You string him along, knowing you'll never let him be with you. He's fated to die for you, too. Just like your mother. Just like everyone around you."

Arryn's entire body tensed even harder as pain ripped its way through her again. She could feel her cheeks growing wet as tears spilled, but she couldn't focus.

Snow? Where was she?

Snow…

The animals…

Elysia had said something about them, but what? It seemed like forever ago, though it had only been minutes.

"Don't bother fighting, sweets. I'm going to make sure you feel every ounce of pain you deserve before you die from your injuries," Scarlett assured her.

But Scarlett had made a mistake.

That Hunter....

Arryn forced her eyes to look up at the man who had shot her. There was no doubt he was one of the Hunters that had killed her mother. She had briefly seen his face in a flash of moonlight as they chased them down that night through the Forest.

But he was *dead*.

Her mother had seen to that. She had died protecting Arryn, but she *had* succeeded. Her mother had killed all the Hunters who had been after them before succumbing to her own wounds. Celine had even confirmed that.

It wasn't real. *He* wasn't real. And if that man standing before her wasn't real, then neither was her wound.

Arryn fought Scarlett as rage filled her. She fed every raw emotion from that night into a seething ball of hatred in her chest and built her power.

She slowly regained her senses. Her companions were still screaming under the onslaught of the other four mystics.

Snow! The moment her familiar's mind connected with hers, she inhaled deeply. When she focused all the mental power she could muster into seeing through Snow's eyes, Scarlett's control weakened.

Arryn now looked down on Scarlett from ten or so feet over her head. *Snow was on top of the Capitol building.*

Scarlett caught a glimpse of what Arryn was seeing, and she whipped around, her eyes darting to the tiger perched above her. With a loud roar, Snow leapt down onto the mystic, which immediately broke her hold on Arryn.

The magically-induced pain vacated her body and she gasped, slowly climbing to her feet. Her eyes turned black and green again as she looked around.

Snow had Scarlett pinned, snapping her massive jaws at the woman, but purposely holding back. Two of the mystics had overwhelmed Elysia, and the other two mentally battered Zoe.

Arryn pulled the energy tight around herself as she allowed it to transport her behind the mystics torturing Elysia. She pulled her daggers from her belt, stabbing each directly through the ribs and into their lungs before pulling the blades free.

She left them alive. In her fury, she wanted them to suffer a slow, painful death for the suffering they had caused so many.

She turned to the two who had attacked Zoe, and their eyes widened as they turned to run. She dropped the daggers and quickly extended her hands to the side as she flexed her entire body, pulling water from the thick, humid air before sending hundreds of jagged shards of ice to pierce their arms and legs while leaving them alive to bleed out on the ground.

Three people were stirring by the main road: Rae, Clara, and Cassondra. They had arrived at some point during the confrontation, only to be subdued with the rest of them.

Go, Clara sent. It was weak, but it was there. *I'm sorry we weren't more help. Take that bitch. We'll heal Elysia and the young mystic.*

Without saying a word, Arryn stalked toward the steps of the Capitol building where Snow had Scarlett trapped. The big cat stepped away as she approached and the mystic flipped onto her stomach, her eyes immediately turning white as she tried to force her way into Arryn's head again.

But it was pointless.

Arryn's emotions had ravaged her and intensified her power, her mind now like a steel fortress. No attack of Scarlett's would get past her shield now.

Scarlett's eyes faded to normal as she tried to back away on her hands and knees, but Snow was in her way. She growled at the woman and nipped at her thigh, causing her to jump forward again. She struggled to her feet, ready to run.

Arryn thrust a hand out, twisting her wrist as she created a rotating wind to pin her in place.

"You have destroyed the lives of so many," Arryn said. "You actually make me miss *Talia*. She was an evil bitch and deserved the end she received, but she didn't have a fucking *thing* on you."

They mystic struggled, so Arryn increased the grip of the wind to the point where the woman couldn't breathe.

"You warped the minds of innocent men and women—people

who will carry the memories of the lives they took, the damage they wrought, long after you're gone."

Scarlett clawed at her throat, and Arryn dropped her, allowing the mystic to breathe.

"Please," Scarlett begged between heaving breaths.

Arryn laughed, taking a step forward. "You know, when I watched the Dark Forest—*my home*—burn, I made a vow to the people who took me in so many years ago. Who taught me respect and loyalty."

The sounds of hundreds of footsteps behind her caught her attention, and she could sense hundreds of people standing there. The battle with the remnant was over, and with the other mystics dead, the compulsion they had been under was gone.

"I promised them I would rip you limb from fucking limb," Arryn said.

The mystic's eyes turned white again, giving it one last shot.

"It wasn't a lie! She's really one of 'em!" an Arcadian behind her shouted.

"Help me!" Scarlett shouted to the crowd, clearly desperate to change her fate. "You see? She's come to take *my* life now! I told you this would happen. There are far more of you than there are of them. Save me!"

Arryn turned to the people behind her, her eyes still fearsome. "Anyone who doesn't want to see this woman die should leave now. I won't let you stop me, but I won't harm you. You should know I'm not leaving until this is done. She *will* pay for what she has done to everyone, druid and Arcadian alike."

Cathillian, Amelia, Celine, and Samuel stepped to the front of the crowd. They looked around, and Samuel took yet another step forward.

"Lass, I think everyone here's realized the truth," he said. "Do it. Do it for the whole Valley."

Everyone began to nod and mumble agreement, many of them shedding tears as they did so or holding the person next to them. She turned to face Scarlett, whose eyes were filled with disbelief.

"Scarlett. It seems the people you manipulated and controlled have sentenced you to die—not that it would have stopped me if they hadn't. For all the people across the Valley who were killed in the remnant attacks, the innocent students at the Academy whose lives were taken, and for all those who died under your rule, I will fulfill my promise."

Scarlett began to shout protests, but Arryn didn't care to hear any more. She thrust her hands forward, vines bursting through the ground as they wrapped around the mystic's limbs and neck.

Pulling her hand back, Scarlett was lifted from the steps and slammed to the flat ground.

"I will not subject these people to even one more drop of blood because of you," Arryn said. "Not even one more horrific memory."

More vines appeared, enveloping Scarlett as she screamed and struggled. Once her body could no longer be seen, Arryn forcefully pulled her hands apart, the vines responding as they ripped Scarlett's body into six separate pieces, the mystic's screams came to an abrupt end.

Sighing, knowing it was over, Arryn relaxed knowing she had fulfilled the vow she made to Cathillian.

Exhausted, Arryn's eyes returned to normal as Cathillian wrapped his arms around her.

"You did it," he said, kissing the top of her head.

Cheers erupted behind them, shocking Arryn. "They've been through a lot," Zoe said as she approached. "The things Scarlett did to them will be there for a while, but right now they're enjoying their freedom. Once the hold is gone…"

Arryn smiled. "I imagine it feels like a hundred-and-twenty-pound weight was lifted."

Zoe nodded. "That's exactly what it feels like. And with

Amelia back, they'll heal. It'll take time, but they'll get their lives back."

Arryn leaned more on Cathillian, both from fatigue and for comfort. He was warm, and her body was chilled from the lingering effects of the mystic's magic and her own magically-induced exhaustion.

"I'm sorry I wasn't able to protect you and Elysia," she said. "She slammed into my head, and I had no idea you were being attacked until you screamed.

Zoe smiled. "Did you really think I came all the way here from the Heights to be completely useless?"

"No," Arryn replied. "I never thought that for a second."

"What she means is, that was the plan the whole time," Elysia said.

Arryn looked at her in confusion, then back to Zoe as the young mystic reached for her hand.

"There were five of them. Scarlett knew you were a huge threat, and she knew we would be distracted—and useless—if anything happened to you. I saw what she planned to do. All five of them were going to go for you, and you alone. They were going to overwhelm you and drive you insane," Zoe said.

"Zoe told me what they had planned, and we agreed we would protect you. We couldn't let them do that to you," Elysia said.

"That was when I told you to go for Scarlett—we had the others. I used my power to make them think we were the much bigger threat, and they attacked us instead of you. It was worth it." Zoe smiled.

Arryn looked at her with wide eyes. "Except you almost died!"

Cathillian squeezed her shoulders. "It's fine. Everyone's fine. Don't worry about that now, okay?"

Snow headbutted Arryn's arm, and she smiled at the big cat as she scratched her colossal head. She had saved Arryn. Had she not taken Scarlett down, Arryn's fate would have been sealed.

"What do we do about *that*?" Arryn asked, gesturing to the dismembered body of Scarlett.

Amelia joined them, several guards behind her. "No worries, my dear. You go and get some rest. I'd recommend staying in Girard's since it hasn't been touched. My house is still a bloody mess from the night I was arrested, so I'll come to you soon myself. As for the bitch, I have a few men who will help me put her exactly where she belongs."

Elysia smiled. "In the sewers with the other one?"

Amelia nodded. "Yup! Let the rats sort it out."

Arryn didn't care much about anything at that moment except sleep. Cathillian lifted her to Snow's back and climbed on as well so he could hold her up.

As they made their way back to Girard's, the house they had called home when they were last in Arcadia, Arryn watched the now-free Arcadian people come together to help bandage the wounded or carry out the bodies of fallen remnant.

It was over. This war was done, and Arcadia was safe again. Only this time, Arryn had a feeling it would be much safer now. Amelia's mental abilities had grown and were continuing to do so, and Arcadia now had the support of the druid warriors of the Dark Forest.

EPILOGUE

Everyone had returned to the Dark Forest, and the governor of Cella had been there, waiting to greet them.

In all his years of leadership, this was the first time the Chieftain had trusted an outsider to oversee the village and the Forest. There had been nothing of note to report—the governor's men had scouted the area, and had kept a close eye on the village and its young and old while they had been gone.

Impressed with the man, his son, and his Guard, and grateful for everything they had helped to accomplish, the Chieftain offered to assist them in rebuilding their city alongside Amelia and any men she provided.

The Chieftain would send enough druids to help grow the trees they would need for construction while Arcadia's men helped build. He planned to do the same thing for Arcadia, after all Amelia had done to protect Arryn and save their home.

He also offered to take on a handful of nature magic students, if the governor could find any who were as pure of heart as he was and they promised to use the magic only for good.

Amelia took back her seat as Chancellor, and immediately began putting a city council in place. She wanted the people to feel they had a say in things instead of being ruled by a single person.

Once Marie and Maddie arrived, Amelia planned to promote her former assistant to the position of Chancellor, while she would become Governor of Arcadia, since they hadn't had one for a long time and the last one had been Adrien's creature. Maddie would be her assistant.

While Marie was both honored and excited to have her new position in the city, she couldn't deny she was most excited to see Andrew. Since they had fled for the Forest, she had been worried senseless about him and was happy to find him safe once the battle was over.

After seeing war happen for a second time within the previous year, she decided taking things slow was overrated.

Instead of returning to Craigston, Samuel had decided to stay in the Dark Forest. He *said* it was for "training" purposes, though Arryn and Cathillian and anyone else with eyes knew it was because Celine had also opted to stay. She wanted to be close to her niece, wherever Arryn chose to live.

While everyone was happy to be back home in the Dark Forest, there was still more to be done before they could rest. There was yet another war on the horizon, and if Corrine was correct, they had only about two weeks to prepare.

That night, everyone gathered around the fire, and wine was passed around by the jug. Everyone planned to get good and drunk with their family and friends.

The Chieftain arrived and sat down in a large chair, holding his usual two mugs of wine. Corrine ran over to sit at his feet, Dante following her. When he caught sight of Arryn, the cub broke away and jumped in her lap, almost immediately rolling over onto his back so she could hold him like a giant baby—his way of requesting tummy rubs.

"Alexander?" Corrine said. She was the only one who called him by his real name, but it didn't seem to bother him at all.

He was quite smitten with the girl. According to Elysia, it was because she reminded him so much of Arryn when she was little. He liked to think he was a wonderful influence. That he was enlightening someone who otherwise would have been led down a path unworthy of their great potential.

"Yes, young one?" the Chieftain replied.

"What happened with you, Alaric, and Jerick? Why do they hate you so much?"

The question was innocent, but not many knew the answer. Druids didn't dwell on the past, though they did hold grudges if there was a great enough betrayal. There were some in the forest who were old enough to remember when Alaric had broken with them, but they didn't talk about it.

"That's a very good question, child," the Chieftain responded. "I suppose, given the circumstances, everyone deserves to know why we are headed into war."

Zoe sat down next to Arryn, giving Dante a scratch. The mystic hadn't yet left, having decided to stay a bit longer and study the druids of the Dark Forest. They interested her greatly, and she wanted to be able to return with more knowledge than she had left with. "Oh! Is it story time?"

Arryn nodded. "The Chieftain is about to tell us what happened with him and the dark druids."

Zoe's eyes lit. "Chieftain?" she blurted out.

He turned to her and smiled. "Yes, young mystic?"

She returned the smile. "If you're going to tell a story, may I assist? At the Temple, I'm a master storyteller. I would love to help."

He thought for a moment before finally nodding. "My stories are always the greatest, but I suppose it couldn't hurt!"

Arryn giggled as she rolled her eyes. The Chieftain never failed to entertain. Cathillian sat down on the other side of her, and she smiled.

"Thanks for saving me a seat," he said.

"I didn't, but you're welcome anyway." She winked.

He leaned toward her and put his mouth next to her ear. "Don't forget," he whispered, "we need to have that talk."

"Don't forget," she whispered back, repeating his words, "we still have another war to get through."

He sat back and nodded. "As long as you haven't forgotten."

She put Dante on the ground before reaching over and grabbing hold of Cathillian's hand. It was a small gesture, but one that seemed to make him feel loved.

Dante ran over to lie down by his new best friend—the equally energetic and rambunctious Corrine.

"So," the Chieftain began. "Everyone of age, grab a mug of wine. With Zoe's help, this should be a pretty good story."

FINIS

Here it is! Another book down! Rounding out the first arc is bittersweet for sure, but I can't tell you how exciting it is! The reviews pouring in have been crazy amazing, the feedback in comments have been motivating, and the level of anticipation the fans show with every book—even though there are a billion other books publishing in the KGU around the same time—is nothing short of awesome.

I just don't know how you guys do it, but I love it! As an indie author, all we ever hear is that book sales are down. People don't read anymore. Well, guess what? Clearly, they aren't surveying the right people. They've never met a KGU fan!

So, this book is very special to me for a lot of reasons. All for the obvious reasons, of course, but there are other reasons I will share as well. Some personal things happened during the writing of this book. A lot of you know from checking out my website that I lost my grandmother recently.

Well, I wanted to take the time to dedicate this book to her. My entire life she rooted for me to succeed. When a lot of parents tell their kids to quit worrying about anything art related, my grandmother was feeding me anything she could to push me.

Her name was Candy McKinley, though her real name was Bessalene. If anyone dared call her that, though, they needed to be ready for a throat punch. She was feisty—a lot like Elysia. She was one of twenty-one (yes, you read that right) children, and all of them were named with B's.

This woman was incredibly talented. She *loved* music and inspired me all the time. She played the guitar (acoustic and electric), banjo, piano, harmonica, accordion, and in her mid-sixties, she took up learning to play the electric bass.

When growing up, I couldn't decide if I wanted to be an author or a rock star—but I think I made the right choice in the end. Ha!

She bought me karaoke machines, gave me instruments, bought me sheet music, and constantly pushed me. That woman never lost hope in me. In my lifetime I've had guitars, drums (though that's the only instrument that *really* stuck with me—I LOVE them!), harmonicas, clarinets, bass, and I'm sure a couple more I forgot. Music has always been a *huge* part of my life, but writing is my passion.

My grandmother always asked questions about it and told me how proud she was. She was so supportive. But because of the KGU, because of all of you, in the last few months of her life, I got to tell her my books were thriving. I got to tell her that my books were a huge success.

She was stuck in bed at home, and she would call her friends and tell them all about it, and she'd call me just to see how many copies I sold. Luckily, Michael keeps us updated often because she asked all the time!

It just excited her to see me succeed. So, I have Michael, the KGU, and all of you to thank for making the last few months of her life an exciting one. That is something I'll hang onto forever.

I shared a story about her in the last book's Author Notes, and she definitely deserved this one. Thank you Mamaw 'Kinley for everything. I love you!

And to end on a less bittersweet note—you guys REALLY went crazy in the reviews!!! Every book I've asked a question for you guys to answer, and the last time I asked what superpower you'd have if you could have one.

Almost all of the reviews answered! That's awesome! It shows you guys are reading these. So, now I want to see you guys tell us what your special talent or dream is/was as a kid. Did you have a special person pushing you along the way?

Thanks again everyone! You guys are the best! Make sure to like the Facebook fan pages for the KGU, The Age of Magic, and my own Candy Crum Books so you get all the cool updates for all of those and my own personal ones, too!

I'll see you guys next time! <3

AUTHOR NOTES - MICHAEL ANDERLE
OCTOBER 25, 2017

First, THANK YOU for not only reading this book, but also reading to the end, past Candy's notes to read mine, as well.

I'm writing this at the JFK airport, after our flight was moved...moved some more and then finally cancelled about seven hours later.

However, we had already moved our ticket and found a clean room. Not a nice room, it was TINY (the kind you step outside to change your mind?) but it was clean.

When I read Candy's notes, I couldn't help but think of my own grandmother, who was one of the biggest supporters in my life. Not that she understood me, but she always loved me. My grandmother is still alive, but her memory is gone. She isn't the same person and doesn't recognize me, which is a little hard.

Even now, this fifty-year old man is tearing up thinking about her and wishing he could wave his BAMAW (Big Ass Magic Author Wand) and change her life.

But I *can't*.

I can tell you that my father, David Anderle, has tried to understand me through my life but our personalities aren't similar. I'm much more of a creative and he is much more of a 'job finisher.'

I would go around, creating all kinds of stuff (usually stuff that doesn't make money) then leaving them when the fun was gone.

His personality is to have everything in its place, and to finish the jobs in front of him. He receives pleasure in 'a job well done.'

I receive pleasure in the creating and figuring out how to accomplish something. Once it is done, my 'fun' slows way down and I'm off to the next creative endeavor. That I've accomplished 20+ books on my own, and over seventy collaborations with other writers, editors, artists etc. is more a testament to my age, than anything else. All of those bosses, mentors, and friends who helped me when I would almost get the job over the finish line.

Occasionally, it was a QC person making sure I finished, or a partner that helped, or a colleague.

However, over the decades finishing the job became ... not easy, but something I worked on. Hell, I'm STILL working on it. I just understand better at fifty that you surround yourself with amazing people that can carry the ball to the goal, if I can get it seventy percent there.

Like Stephen Campbell, who will take these author notes, marry them with Candy's and the story, the edited JIT notes (thank you all!) and the editor / artists for the cover and produce this book.

Hell, just thinking about it makes me realize what a fantastic team of people we have working to produce these books.

I'm truly, truly blessed to be working with people from around the world to make this a reality.

And in the end, all of you have provided my father a chance to realize that his often 'odd' son had something special in him the whole time. It just took the world, and the vision of Jeff Bezos and those at Amazon to provide him a platform to get the stories out of his brain.

My father has seen when I ranked #24 in the store, and as the #1 Best Seller in Science Fiction. While my grandmother won't know that, even though she still lives, I know that she loved me no matter how 'unique' I was to every one else.

So, I dedicate this book to my Grandmother, Lillie J. Anderle who was the earliest one to just accepted the uniqueness that was in me.

I owe all of my parents (David & Jo Lynn, and Marlene) for raising me to be a *good guy*. They taught me to respect the law and those in the military by doing so themselves. (Even when my Dad was pulled over for speeding – he might bitch in private, but he was respectful in person.)

To all of those who came before us, we thank you for your support in making us who we are today.

Ad Aeternitatem,
Michael Anderle

BOOKS BY CANDY CRUM

TALES OF THE FEISTY DRUID

with Michael Anderle

The Arcadian Druid (01) - The Undying Illusionist (02) - The Frozen
Wasteland (03) - The Deceiver (04) - The Lost (05) - The Damned (06)
Into The Maelstrom (07)

THE THERIAN CHRONICLES

with Amanda Browning

The Dark Professor (1) The Therian Prince (2)

BOOKS BY MICHAEL ANDERLE

For a complete list of books by Michael Anderle, please visit

www.lmbpn.com/ma-books/

All LMBPN Audiobooks are Available at Audible.com and iTunes. For a complete list of audiobooks visit:

www.lmbpn.com/audible

CONNECT WITH THE AUTHORS

To see ALL of Candy's different books check out her website below

Website:
http://www.candycrumbooks.com

Facebook
https://www.facebook.com/groups/thecandyshopgroup/

Michael Anderle Social

Website:
http://www.lmbpn.com

Email List:
http://lmbpn.com/email/

www.ingramcontent.com/pod-product-compliance
Lightning Source LLC
Chambersburg PA
CBHW050246110726
47898CB00007B/2295